MW01680199

Snake in the Grass

A Marco Mystery -- Book 1

"Marco is a charming narrator with a nose for mystery. A delightful reminder that our four-footed friends know more about human nature than we do. Read this with your dog curled up at your feet. But don't tell the cat."

Rebecca Cantrell, New York Times best-selling author

Snake in the Grass

A Marco Mystery -- Book 1

A man in mourning. A lost dog.

Join the newest crime-fighting duo on their first intriguing adventure.

In this enchanting first entry in the Marco Mystery series, Coleman Steele, barely recovering from his wife's death, and Marco, a dog searching for his family, team up to help a friend in need.

As the man and his new little pal follow an increasingly complicated trail, they enter the bizarre world of the super-rich where they encounter liars, con-artists, and killers.

Cole has been hiding away in his small compound in Portland, Oregon, for a year following the death of his wife. Marco has been searching for his family for who knows how long before fetching up at Cole's front gate.

Soon after his arrival Marco persuades Cole to help Elena Ortega, Cole's gardener and friend, find her missing brother, Javier. The search begins on Sauvie Island in the Columbia River, where the ultra-wealthy Bloomfields reside. The family is so adept at guarding their secrets that lying is second nature. With every misleading statement they derail Cole and Marco's quest to find the missing man.

Following a family tragedy, connected to Javier's disappearance, the Bloomfields close ranks, spew lies, and steer Cole and Marco onto dangerous ground.

When Marco shows Cole that he's a crack investigator, as well as a loving companion, a brilliant partnership is born.

SNAKE IN THE GRASS

A Marco Mystery

Kathryn Wadsworth

Mystery Bay Publishing

Thank you, Danielle - you are such a bright spirit full of love and enthusiasm.

♡ KBW

A Mystery Bay Publications Original, November 2018

Copyright © 2018 by Kathryn Wadsworth.

Wadsworth, Kathryn. Snake in the Grass. Mystery Bay Publishing Print Edition. Cover design: David Deardorff

Snake in the Grass is a work of fiction. Names, places, and incidents either are products of the author's imagination or are used fictitiously. Any resemblance to actual events, locales, or persons, living or dead, is entirely coincidental.

Mystery Bay Publishing ISBN: 978-0-9894683-4-3

All rights reserved. Published in the United States by Mystery Bay Publishing, 2023 East Sims Way, # 170, Port Townsend, Washington, 98368.

Contact us at:
Facebook:
https://www.facebook.com/mysterybaypublishing/
Kathryn@kathrynanddavid.com

For David and Frodo
My real-life Cole and Marco
the best mates a woman could have.

SNAKE IN THE GRASS

A Marco Mystery

Prologue

The Columbia River snakes its way through canyons, past islands, sandy shores, grasses, forests, and farms. It coils toward the sea as it nears the Oregon coast, luring sea gulls inland. Soaring above the murky water, the gulls watch for prey below.

Early morning light glints off the river's surface and hits the glass tabletop perched on the sandy clearing. The gulls swoop. Startled, they shriek at the hulking man with the blood-red tie sitting at the table.

The man's arms windmill, scattering the birds. "Get away," he shrieks, ducking his head. He swivels right and left to see if anyone witnessed his terror. He sees no one.

The watcher ducks behind thick shrubs and tall grasses, hiding on the nearly overgrown trail, and snickers at the big man's fear. The small man is late, and the watcher is impatient, tired of waiting for the right moment.

The young, dark-skinned man finally arrives, stumbling across the shifting sand. He trudges up the grass-covered hummock, hesitates, shielding his eyes against the rising sun that flashes off the water. He tilts his head, slaps his hand against his thigh.

Irritated. Good.

The crouching spy creeps closer to the river. Staying out of sight but moving closer to the gazebo that hunkers over the table in the clearing. The fat man in a dark blue suit now sits quietly at the square table with ebony legs that support the thick glass. His bright red tie streams like a ribbon of lava from his neck to his crotch.

Pretentious prick.

The man at the table fidgets, plunging the filter on his glass French-press coffee pot. He flips a page from the stack of papers in front of him.

Crossing to the gazebo, the small dark man, wearing jeans and a denim work shirt, pauses beside the table. He speaks, but the watcher cannot hear what he says. The seated man gestures for the new-comer to sit, then pours out two cups of coffee. The two men talk while they paw through the papers on the table.

The big man smacks the table, scattering the papers to the ground. The other man leans back, shaking his head.

"You goddamn liar," the big man bellows.

The watcher smiles.

Both men sit motionless. Neither speaks. Moments tick by. The small man leans forward, takes a sip of coffee. He grimaces, sets the glass mug down on the table. They converse quietly.

What are they talking about? Patience is called for.

The small man stands and walks to the outdoor kitchen along one edge of the gazebo. He removes a canister of beans from the shelf above the coffee maker. He rotates the canister, examining the contents.

The big man suddenly rises, knocking his chair to the ground. The watcher races to him, shoving him in the back. Crying out, the fat man stumbles forward and falls, striking his head on the table. He does not move.

The man by the coffee maker turns toward the watcher and the man on the ground.

Blood oozes onto the sand from the big man's mouth.

Marco Diary Entry 1

I don't know how long I've been on the run. So long I've almost forgotten my old life. I do remember snuggles from the children, decent meals every morning, the alphas coming home every evening when I sit on the couch between them. But when they pack up our things and drive away, they put the little boy in charge. When we stop two days later, he loses me. Now I keep moving from place to place, one step ahead of people who want to lock me up.

This compound looks nice. Quiet, off the street, and private. A good place to hide. But I can't get through the fence, and I'm too tired to go on. I'll just curl up here against the gate and rest a bit. No one is out at this hour anyway. Not even the dog catcher. I should be okay. I'll sleep a little. But only for a minute. I can't let anyone see me. I have to leave before the sun comes up. My entire family is missing, and I must keep searching.

* * *

I wake with a start. It's still night. A man meanders up the sidewalk toward me. He's moving slow, weaving, and humming. He's wearing fancy clothes, but alcohol fumes come off him in waves. I know that smell from the alleys where I forage for food. I don't like it.

When he gets close, I growl. Low in my throat, just loud enough to let him know not to come any closer. But he keeps walking. Maybe he doesn't see me. Or hear me. But then he bends over to look at me. I sit up on my haunches, bare my teeth, and bark. Just once to let him know I'm not kidding.

He squats a couple of feet away, then holds out his hand so I can smell his fingers. People aren't usually that polite. I give them a sniff.

"Hey, little buddy." He doesn't yell at me like most people do. He bares his teeth, but in that way people do when they're trying to be friendly.

He touches me lightly on the top of my head. I flinch. I don't mean to, but I do. I wag my tail to let him know I'm not really afraid.

"It's okay, little guy." The man caresses my neck and side, then sits beside me and leans against the gate too. "You're safe."

We sit quietly in the hazy twilight before sunrise. Though I can still smell the booze and scent trails of dozens of other people on his clothes, he seems to be at peace, happy to do nothing more than sit here with me.

But that's not the whole story. I can tell he has a troubled heart.

He draws in a deep breath and turns to look me in the eye. "Want to come home with me?"

I crawl into his lap and give his fingers one quick lick. He obviously needs me, and I feel I can trust him. For the moment, at least. Maybe he'll give me some breakfast before I head out to find my family. With a full belly for a change.

He lifts me as he stands, swiftly, in one graceful movement. He moves effortlessly. Maybe he's a dancer. Or an athlete. He reaches into his pocket for a set of keys. Flicking through them slowly he finds the one he's looking for and opens the gate.

Chapter One

The night Cole found the dog he was walking home from a party at his pal, Isabelle's, pop-up speakeasy. He'd co hosted a fund-raiser for one of the local rescue shelters. First time he'd been out in a long time. Despite his year-long aversion to social activities, it was important to share his good fortune, such as it was. His invention had made him rich, and he couldn't just hoard it. Especially now.

Birds were beginning to stir in the soft light before dawn. Cole liked that time of day when he had the streets mostly to himself. He'd had a lot to drink but wasn't stumbling down the sidewalk or anything. He was just high enough to dull the pain and content enough to be alive. After the last horrible year, since Christine's death, that had to be good enough.

The pooch was a gray tangled mop of matted hair, twigs, leaves, and dirt that night. But once he was washed and groomed, he turned out to be a white curly-haired Bichon Frise. To Cole the pup looked pure-bred, like the ones online. A little more research revealed that Bichons had been bred as companions and to accompany sailors on long voyages.

Cole looked down at the dog nestled in his lap. "So, you're a sailor like me." Cole had grown up on a sailboat and served in the navy when he'd dropped out of college, but he saw no need to explain that to the dog.

A trip to the vet showed the dog was in pretty good health, though underweight. He wore no collar, and there was nothing else to identify him. Cole had him vaccinated, got him new dog tags, and a micro-chip registered in the name of Coleman Steele.

He hadn't had a dog since he was a boy, and that had been a schipperke, so coming up with a good name beyond Skipper was a challenge. He wanted to give the dog a name that fit. What the hell, the pooch seemed right at home.

Cole squatted. "What's your name anyway? What am I going to call you?"

The dog just stared at him.

"I can't read your mind, Buddy, try as I might." Cole thought it over. "Well, you're quite the wanderer. How about Marco Polo? Yeah, Marco for short. That's a good name for a wanderer."

The pup wagged his tail and licked Cole's face. Good enough.

Food was pretty important to the dog. He hung around the communal kitchen, keeping an eye on Cole's private chef, Nicholas. That made sense, as he'd clearly been starving for quite some time before he fetched up at Cole's compound. He also seemed to want to earn his keep and gave himself a number of jobs. Primarily, assistant gardener and chief of surveillance.

He apprenticed himself to the gardener, Elena, observing everything she did. When he wasn't with her, he stationed himself by the front gate and watched the street. He commented on everything he saw with a short bark. If anyone came to the gate and hit the button for the intercom, he eyed them with suspicion. And whenever someone he didn't know actually entered the grounds, he followed them everywhere, watching everything they did.

Then he'd check back with Cole to make sure it was allowed. Cole would nod, tell him it was okay, and he'd go back to his surveillance.

Marco Diary Entry 2

The compound is even better than I guessed from the street that night. Everyone who lives here is kind to me, and clearly the man needs me. I spend the first few days trying to find a way out, just in case things don't work out. I postpone my trek to find my family, at least for now. It's been a long time since I saw them. I know they love me, and I love them, but they lost me. And so far, this place isn't so bad.

Everyone calls the alpha male Cole. He's the one who found me. He's tall and lean, but strong with a square jaw and pleasing face. A tattoo wraps around his right arm from wrist to shoulder. It looks like some kind of bird. His eyes are blue, like a husky's. His black hair is short on the sides, but long on top and sometimes falls down over his eyes. I don't like it when I can't see his eyes.

It seems he owns all the homes behind the gate here. The other people who live here work for him. He goes out at night, coming home smelling of booze and cannabis and many different men and women. I guess he must be looking for a new mate, because I hear the others say there used to be an alpha female, but she's gone. I can smell his grief, though no one speaks of it to him. He often sleeps most of the morning, then goes for a run or works out in his private gym, has lunch, and spends the afternoon in his garden. But he never goes anywhere to work.

The garden is where I hang out. It's big, with lots of open space, and lots of trees and shrubs to poop behind, though the gardener always comes along and picks it up. Cole calls her Elena, and she takes care of the whole garden, not just my poop. She's a small dark woman with black, curly hair and an easy smile. She wears jeans and t-shirts and a tool belt with trowels and clippers and other gardening gadgets.

I help her as much as I can. I dig up weeds whenever she does and pull up grass that grows next to the flower beds with my teeth. A tip I'll share with you: grass is a good snack for a starving dog. I also do frequent perimeter checks to keep an eye on things, and exchange pee-mail with dogs that walk by outside the fence.

Cole is mostly interested in the flowers. He and Elena spend hours talking about them. I don't know how these two could have so much to say, but I smell each flower carefully and commit each one's scent to memory in case Cole and Elena ever need to talk to me about them. There's also good food I can pick, like kale and kohlrabi. Carrots and strawberries are my favorites. I really like sweets.

When Elena and I harvest vegetables, we take them to Nicholas, Cole's chef, who lives in the last house at the back of the property. He's a huge man with long sandy brown hair pulled into dreadlocks, and wiry stubble across his face. His light brown skin is covered in tattoos, and he has small gleaming blobs of shiny metal stuck in his ears and nose and eyebrows. He's also very loud. At first, he scared me because he reminded me of some of the men I used to see in the alleys. But Nicholas makes me really good food, and when his wife, Shannon, comes home from work, she takes me in her lap and kisses me and feeds me special treats from the table. She has pale skin, long red hair, and green eyes. They say she's a lawyer, and she's even bigger and louder than Nicholas. She seems very powerful, and I think Nicholas is a little bit afraid of her.

They all talk a lot at dinner. And I listen. It's a good idea to know as much as possible about the people you live with. I am relieved to hear that Cole owns a prosperous outdoor equipment and adventure travel company. He also invented something the military buys that makes him a lot of money. That's good. He's not likely to run out of dog food. But he doesn't work at his company anymore. That has something to do with the absence of the alpha female, but they skip that part of the story. Sometimes I hear more about it when he's gone, so that's how I know she's dead. When Cole's home for dinner, we all eat at the long table in his country kitchen in the middle of the compound. Everyone tells stories and laughs.

Yeah, I think I'll stay for a while.

Chapter Two

Marco had been with Cole for a couple of weeks when early one morning he came over and poked Cole in the calf with his nose. Cole bent over and gave him a pat but kept moving. Since the pup had moved in, Cole had begun to rise early and go for a morning run. This morning he was in a hurry to get moving before joining Elena in the garden.

Marco poked him again.

"What's up, boy?" Cole crouched to look at him.

Marco looked back with a steady gaze.

"C'mon, little buddy." Cole stood and continued toward the back gate.

The dog stopped and stared.

"Okay. Let's go, Marco."

He trotted beside Cole, but soon stopped again and barked. When Cole looked back, Marco ran in circles, and then headed toward the garden shed, barking wildly, and looking back over his shoulder. What was that about? Cole followed. He wanted to talk to Elena about the strawberry patch, anyway. Some of the plants were in big trouble and he didn't know what was up.

They found her in the potting shed. Crying. Uh-oh. Cole stopped in the doorway. He was not eager to intrude. To be honest he did not want to go anywhere near a crying woman. No matter what the trouble was.

Not Marco. He walked right past Cole and stood on his hind legs, pawing at her thigh with his front feet.

She looked down, wiping her eyes with a sleeve.

"Hey, sweet one." She bent down but startled when she saw Cole standing in the doorway.

"Oops. Sorry." Cole turned away and stepped back outside before she said anything to him.

Marco ran past Cole, slipping through the door, and stopped right in front of him. Cole stepped around the dog. Marco did it again. "Okay. Okay." Cole turned back, like the dog wanted him to.

Elena stood at the potting bench at the far end of the shed, sorting through some of the organic remedies they kept on hand. The shed was big and bright. Light shone through windows that opened to let in fresh air, and shelving under the windows held fertilizers, organic remedies, and hand tools.

Her back was to Cole, so he cleared his throat. When she turned Cole asked her about the strawberries. Yeah, he was a coward. They got into a discussion about the problem and her options for dealing with it. She said it was likely red stele disease, and she'd probably have to dig up the ailing plants to get them out of the garden.

"Okay, I'll let you get on with it." Cole started out the door.

Marco barked. Just once, a sharp yelp. Then he stared at Cole again. He still couldn't read the dog's mind but was beginning to get the message. Cole was well aware that the pup was trying to use mind control to tell Cole to shape up. Okay. Okay.

Cole turned to Elena. "What can I do to help?"

She took a deep breath. Her eyes widened, but she smiled. "It's my brother."

Cole nodded. She had two brothers, but only talked about one, Javier. She never mentioned the other one, Tony. Lots of bad feeling there, but Cole had never asked her about it. Seemed like it was none of his business.

Javier managed the gardens at the Bloomfield estate, over on Sauvie Island, in the middle of the Columbia River a few miles north of Portland. Partly a working farm, partly a private home with lush grounds, the estate was open to the public only one day a year – the 4th of July. Some kind of patriotic statement, Cole assumed. He knew the current owner, but not well. They attended the same charity balls, sat on some of the same foundation boards, but neither of them was very active, and they had only a nodding acquaintance.

"I'm sorry," Cole said again, not sure he wanted to hear more. Pretty sure he didn't, actually.

"They fired him last week." Her eyes watered, and she looked down at her feet. "Now, he's gone."

"What do you mean, gone?" Awkward.

She looked at Cole like he was some kind of fool. "Javier's disappeared. He said he was coming over. Five days ago. He never showed up."

"Maybe he just went somewhere to clear his head." Cole wasn't about to ask her if she'd called Javier on his cell or gone to his house. He didn't want to get another of those looks.

"He would have called me." Her voice quavered. "No matter what. I think something has happened to him."

"Do you know what might have happened?" Well, that sounded just as stupid.

She shook her head.

"Do you know why he was fired?"

She looked at Cole the way Marco did when he wanted one of the treats Cole carried in his pocket.

"You know him. Mr. Bloomfield, I mean. Could you ask him? Find out what happened?"

Aw, hell. Cole didn't want to get involved, but now he had to. Damn that dog.

Marco Diary Entry 3

Cole tells Elena he will help her. Good. I like Elena. She's gentle and smart, but unsure of herself. She works hard to prove she knows what she's doing. I love helping her in the garden. She always talks to me while she works. I learn a lot from her. We're good pals.

The garden beds, where she grows the food, are on the other side of the compound from Cole's two-story brick house. His house is tucked away in a private corner of the compound. It's separated from the rest by a mowed lawn surrounded by colorful flowers on big mounds that stretch across the center of the property. Elena keeps everything neat and tidy, and, of course, I help. The grounds are not as wild as I would like. But I hear Cole and Elena talking about making it more natural. I can't wait to see what they do.

Even though I prefer wild places, a wilder garden will make my job more difficult. I am the only one concerned about security. I find Cole's attitude pretty negligent. I have to check every visitor, and then do what I can to alert Cole. He hardly ever pays attention, and I think he is altogether too easy-going about potential threats. Big men dressed in overalls that unload boxes from big, square trucks that rumble up and down the street. Highly suspect, if you ask me. Which Cole doesn't. I have to look out for him and all the others I live with - Nicholas, Shannon, and Elena. They're careless too. But Cole is the boss so he's the one who needs to know what's going on. My point is - while I pal around with Elena, I must still be vigilant.

You should know this about Elena -- even when we are working hard, she always remembers my lunch time and goes with me to the large communal kitchen where Nicholas makes special food for me. He says dogs shouldn't eat people food all the time, and that we need special nutrition. I disagree. I think people food is great, but whatever he makes is delicious. When we're all together in the evening they share their food with me. Sometimes they do at lunch time too.

Now I follow Cole as he stalks back toward his house, but instead of going straight there he veers off toward the greenhouse. It has clear walls and roof and is home to hundreds of odd plants with big, fluffy or sometimes strange spiky flowers. Cole calls them orchids, and he takes very special care of them. Some flowers have really bright colors. Others have arching sprays that reach the floor. I like walking the aisles with Cole and sniffing each one. Some smell wonderful, and some have no scent at all.

I often spend time here with Cole and Elena. It's one of my favorite spots. Here's how I first learned about this place - Cole takes me for my medical check-up and I get way too many shots. Then he takes me to this other woman who seems nice. But it's a dirty trick. She gets me soaking wet, washes me, and then cuts almost all my hair off. I'm afraid he might leave me there. But he comes back to get me. He brings me here to this wonderful hot house where I can warm up. The heat reminds me of where I used to live.

So, I hang out here with the orchids when I get the chance, which isn't too often because, like I say, I have a lot of work to do. When we're here I listen to Cole and Elena talk about the plants. I notice how different their voices are – Elena's sounds like the music my family used to sing.

Cole's is slower, steadier, and less fluid. No matter how they speak, I can tell they love these flowers. So, I do too.

Now Cole walks up and down the aisles muttering. I can tell he's not talking to me, so I trot over to the plants with the big, ruffled flowers and sniff them all. Some smell like perfume. One reminds me of the alpha female where I used to live. The scent makes me happy to think about her and sad because I miss her so much.

Cole sits down on the ground and holds his head in his hands. He needs me, so I trot over to him and lick his face. He pets my side and I lean against his leg.

"Christine would have loved you, Marco." He sighs, his eyes closed. He leans over and whispers in my ear. "It's all my fault you know. I should have stopped her."

We sit close in the quiet fragrance of flowers for a long time. Finally, Cole stands, wipes his face and we go back to his house. We skip our morning run.

Chapter Three

Cole usually walked or rode his bicycle or took the light rail, but to get to Sauvie Island he had to drive. That was not entirely true. He could have taken the bus, but it would have taken forever. Besides he wanted to bring Marco.

Cole's place encompassed about an acre on the edge of the city on the hillside just below Washington Park in Northwest Portland. He'd spent a small fortune on renovations to make it state of the art "green." He didn't own a car, so he called to reserve one of the share-cars parked down the street.

The night before he'd also called Bloomfield and, though he was surprised to hear from Cole, he was gracious enough when Cole invited himself over for morning coffee. Donald was always genial, a burly guy with a "hail-fellow-well-met" demeanor. He told funny jokes. Cole liked him but was wary. His radar told him Bloomfield was not entirely trustworthy, so Cole generally kept his distance.

Cole left home as soon as possible to avoid commuter traffic. He thought it was early enough, but it was a lost cause. An accident on the 405 had brought everything to a standstill. He called Donald from the car to let him know he was running late. Donald had a good laugh at Cole's expense but didn't seem to mind.

Cole was an hour late when he pulled up to the security gate at the estate. He pushed the buzzer but got no response. He waved at the security camera. Still nothing. He called Donald on his cell, but there was no answer, so Cole left a message, apologizing for being late and asking Donald to get someone to open the gate. The only reason Cole stuck around was because he felt sorry for Elena. What should he try next?

Cole stared at the security camera for a while, but that got boring pretty quick, so he left the car to look for another way in. He clipped Marco's leash to his halter and started walking on the faint trail that paralleled the walled perimeter. They followed it a good half mile or so, but never saw an opening. Cole could have climbed the eight-foot tall wall, but what would he have done with Marco? The car was in full sun so leaving him there was not an option. Besides, climbing the wall could get Cole arrested for trespassing, although he doubted Donald would call the cops.

Cole really didn't think an hour behind schedule should get him ostracized, but maybe in Bloomfield world it did. He tried to picture the extent of the property. He'd been there at a party last year, with his wife. The working farm was further downstream with its own service entrance. Extensive gardens surrounded the house, buffering it from the farm.

The house overlooked the beach that ran along the Columbia River. They'd watched fishing boats and tugs towing barges steam past while VIPs gave speeches asking for money to fund more ways to help salmon and other wildlife. After the speeches a string quartet played while the guests scarfed smoked salmon and guzzled champagne. The irony was not lost on him or on Christine. They'd laughed all the way to their new home.

But first the two of them had walked along the river listening to the murmur of flowing water. Just around a bend, out of sight from the house, they'd come upon a clearing with a lovely beach pavilion. A café table and two chairs sat in the middle of the pavilion, and a small outdoor kitchen ran along one side. They sat, holding hands, listening to the river and the faint sounds of the music behind them. Seemed like the perfect place for a little private kiss. The wine encouraged them, and one thing led to another.

Okay. Enough. He wasn't going to think about that.

He walked a little further, curious about whether the wall ran all the way to the river. Could he simply walk around the end of it and down the beach? He'd still be trespassing, so probably not a great idea.

That was that. He turned back. He'd tell Elena the whole thing was a bust. He wasn't going to get inside. Maybe someone in her family or one of his friends could tell her where Javier was.

At the gate a security guard leaned against the hood of Cole's car. He had blocked Cole in with his own ride, tricked out to look like a police cruiser. So much for getting out of this gracefully. At this point Cole didn't care how he backed out, with poise or ineptitude. To be out was good enough.

Cole walked over and leaned against the hood next to the guard. Marco hung back, pulling on his leash so that he was as far away from them as possible. Cole looked at the man's badge and read his name. It seemed vaguely familiar.

"Officer Ordway, how's your day going?" Cole was shooting for affable, but knew he sounded snotty because he wondered why the guy wanted to box him in. It wasn't like he was actually on the estate yet. Maybe Ordway thought being in the driveway encroached on his territory.

"Better than yours, I'm guessing."

Oh yeah, Cole remembered him. He'd chased Christine and Cole off the shore that night. Ordway struck Cole as kind of a jerk, but maybe that's how the man saw his job. Keeping the riff raff off the beach.

Cole smiled at him. "I've got an appointment with Donald, but no one answered the buzzer." It was time Cole stopped wasting everyone's time, especially his own.

The security guard grunted. "Ever hear of a cell phone?"

"Oh yeah? What's that?" What a jack-ass. Cole realized maybe he was being the jackass. He made an attempt to be more charitable. Maybe the guy was just naturally zealous. Or maybe he was on thin ice with his boss. "Tried it. No answer."

The man squinted in Cole's direction. "I'm guessing Mr. Bloomfield changed his mind."

"Maybe so." Cole shrugged, opened the car door, and guided Marco into the passenger seat. Walking around the car, Cole got into the driver's seat, relieved to have an excuse to give Elena, and get out of his hasty commitment. "Guess I'll head out then." Cole started the car.

Ordway looked ahead at the gate but made no move.

Huh. Cole lowered his window and stuck his head out. "Something else on your mind?"

The guard turned and glowered at Cole. He searched his memory. Had he done something last year to piss the guy off? He couldn't think of a thing. Ordway looked at his watch, then heaved forward, hoisting his ass off the hood of Cole's car.

When he passed the open window, he gave Cole a brief wave. "See ya, Mr. Steele." He got in the front seat of his cruiser and sat still.

There was just enough room to inch Cole's car forward a few feet, then jockey back and forth, maneuvering his car so he could get out. Just as Cole slipped the car into reverse to finally make his escape, the gate slid open. He shifted to drive, pressed the accelerator and shot through the opening onto the estate grounds.

As soon as he was through, the gate slid shut behind him. Cole gave Ordway a jaunty wave as he and Marco made their way toward the house. Cole laughed. He couldn't help himself.

Marco Diary Entry 4

Cole steers the car along a gravel drive. I hear the stones popping under the tires and smell the river beyond the tall trees and the big house. We pass under towering trees that line a wide road until we reach a broad parking area of paving stones. They sound different from the gravel. The empty parking area is bordered by flower beds that look a lot like our place. Maybe that's because Javier is Elena's brother and he is in charge of the gardens here. Maybe gardens like this run in their family like white hair in mine.

Cole stops the car beside a huge stone building with ten big garage doors along the front. He clips my leash to my halter – he doesn't know yet that he doesn't need to do that all the time – and opens the door for me. I carefully inspect each blade of grass as we make our way toward a massive house, with broad steps leading to a gigantic portico. All the buildings are made from the same sandy-colored stone.

I smell for scents left by others. It could be useful. I find faint traces of various odors that I need to investigate. One smells familiar. Like Elena. I bet it's Javier. Another scent trail smells like the man at the gate. He passed this way earlier this morning. I don't recognize the other people who have walked here. Some are male, some female. That's all I know so far.

I hear voices. Barely audible. I stop and prick up my ears. I look at Cole. I can tell he can't hear them. But I know whoever they are, they're shouting.

Chapter Four

Cole rang the bell. And waited. Again. The business at the gate was weird. Why had there been no answer? Wasn't anyone on the security team assigned to answer the intercom? Bloomfield expected Cole, so why had no one let him in? And, since Ordway knew his name – which was odd – why hadn't he opened the gate? Wasn't that part of his job?

Cole shook his head. The vagaries of the rich and powerful. Cole was only recently rich, so it was all foreign to him. It seemed inefficient. He bet tradesmen came and went in an altogether different location, through a gate not nearly so grand.

He rang the bell again, and then pounded on the door. Maybe the bell was broken. What the hell was going on here? He had yet to see a human being, if you didn't count Ordway, and Cole admitted the guy barely registered on any meter.

Marco sat calmly beside Cole, looking into his face and wagging his tail, then turning to stare at the closed door. He looked at Cole again, then back at the door. Marco barked once, sharply. Gave Cole another look, one that he swore was incredulous, as though the pup were asking, "Can you believe how rude these people are?"

Cole laughed out loud.

The door opened abruptly, flung back by a man who shouted over his shoulder down the hallway, "Shut up."

He turned back to Cole and startled, as though he had not expected anyone to be there. The man wore a gray tailored suit and a silk tie with red and white stripes. His black hair bristled in a military cut on his perfectly round head. His eyes, the color of glacial ice, seemed to look right through Cole.

Neither man spoke.

The man turned suddenly and marched back down the hall, leaving the door wide open. Cole followed. Weirder and weirder. Cole didn't shut the door, either. Just in case he and Marco needed a quick exit.

The guy led the way into a cavernous formal sitting room. A hideous empty fireplace stretched across one wall, its golden mantel protruding three feet into the room. Three women, their knees nearly touching, sat in gilt chairs clustered in front of the cold fireplace. A vast, intricate oriental carpet covered the oak floors, but otherwise the room was barren. It hadn't been so sparsely furnished a year ago.

"I told you," one of the women hissed to the others, "that is not going to happen."

Marco growled, low in his throat. All three women turned to glare at Cole and Marco. It seemed as though they'd interrupted an argument of some kind.

The hissing woman stood and crossed the room. Auburn hair, scarlet lips, carmine dress, spiked ruby heels. Four different shades, but all of them red. She smiled abruptly and extended her hand.

"Good morning. So good of you to come. I'm Portia Bloomfield." She paused, the smile frozen where she'd left it. "And you are?"

Marco sat down beside Cole and made no move to greet her. Highly unusual.

"Coleman Steele." Cole held out his hand and she took it. "We met at the Salmon Safe fund-raiser last year."

"Of course." Her pale green eyes were completely blank, and Cole realized she had no memory of meeting him. But then, why would she? There were hundreds of people there. Of course, he'd gotten a card from her after Christine's death, but more likely an assistant had done that. "What can I do for you?"

"I was supposed to meet your father an hour ago, but I got held up in traffic. Is he here?" Cole looked from one to another of the three women, but there was no response. They were like zombies, the Stepford Wives. Decidedly creepy.

"I'm trying to find Javier Ortega." The women did not respond, as though they hadn't heard him. "He works here." He added, just in case.

One of the two who had remained seated leapt to her feet and left the room. Brenda was her name, Cole recalled. A younger sister. The other sister, whose name Cole could not remember, rose slowly, clasped her hands in front of her breast, and bowed her head, as if in prayer.

Marco held perfectly still beside Cole.

"Krista," Portia walked over to her. "Please go ask Brenda to call papa on his cell." She stressed the second syllable of papa with a thick and sudden French accent. "He must be around here somewhere."

Portia turned back to face Cole as Krista left the room. "You remember Brenda's husband, Blake, don't you, Mr. Steele?" She gestured to the man who had opened the door to let Cole and Marco in.

Cole said he did, though he didn't. In fact, he had not met any of these people before, aside from Portia. But he remembered her well. Aggressively in charge of the gala, dictating each moment as if the guests were soldiers, gathering for a review by the commander in chief. Turned out the commander in chief for the evening was her father.

"I'll go find Donald. I think I know where he is." Blake strode from the room.

Marco stood and walked to the end of the leash, trying to follow him out the door. Portia said no more. Cole excused himself and went with Marco. It was a relief.

Blake was long gone, as if he'd run for all he was worth as soon as he got out of Portia's sight. Cole didn't blame the guy. Maybe Javier wasn't missing at all but had fled this bizarro world. He might be well out of it.

Cole headed toward the back of the house to find a door that led outside. Donald had an office somewhere, but Cole had heard he liked to spend most of his time wheeling and dealing from his riverside pavilion. The one Christine and Cole had discovered - much to Ordway's disapproval.

Cole crossed the patio and set out in the direction that Marco pulled. Upriver. Cole trotted to keep pace. Marco started the yipping and bounding he did when he picked up the scent of a deer. He'd reached the end of his leash, and he looked like a rabbit hopping in place. Cole kept up a steady pace and let the dog lead the way.

They crossed over lawns with grass on the edge of being too long, dodged around perennial borders where weeds began to peek above the mulch. Cole glimpsed the tall row of poplars down river that separated the estate from the working farm.

Continuing upriver they rounded a bend, and Cole spotted the pavilion on the beach. Marco pulled even harder, and Cole ran flat out. He'd finally caught the dog's sense of urgency. Cole stopped at the edge of the clearing where the pavilion stood. Marco kept running and nearly pulled the leash from his hand. Donald lay in the sand. Blood pooled around his mouth.

Marco Diary Entry 5

I keep running even though I am not getting anywhere. Cole stops and holds my leash so tight I can't pull away from him. I lift my head, pricking up my ears and sniffing the breeze that brings the man's scent to me. I smell and hear things Cole can't. I've learned that people can't sense what I can. I bark once, sharply, to get Cole's attention. We need to act quickly. I hear the man's breath, very faint. I smell his life ebbing away.

Chapter Five

Cole reached for his cell and dialed 9-1-1. He asked for an ambulance immediately but figured it would take a while to get out to the island. He'd trained in first aid in the military, but Donald looked way past first aid. Cole had studied and occasionally had to perform emergency wilderness medicine when he ran trips in remote areas. He'd also investigated crimes in the navy, and he didn't want to make a mess of things for the forensics team.

While Cole weighed the pros and cons, Marco had no doubts. He barked, looked at Cole, and barked again. He pulled Cole toward Donald. The pup knew Cole had to do something. He was right, but Cole moved cautiously to avoid disturbing the scene. He shortened Marco's retractable leash to keep him close.

Donald lay stretched out beside the café table on his back, his head turned to the side. He clutched a blood-spattered cloth napkin in his right hand. An empty French press coffee pot, wet grounds pooling in the bottom, sat in the middle of the table. Two espresso cups – one empty, one full - sat beside the pot. Both of the chairs Cole had seen last year were pulled up to the table.

Donald was pale, except for a round reddish patch on his forehead. When Cole touched the man's wrist, searching for a pulse, his skin was cold and clammy. Could Cole feel a flutter? He tried the carotid artery. He looked for the rise and fall of the chest and held his palm under the man's nose. Yes, Cole felt faint signs of life.

"Donald." Cole spoke softly. "Can you hear me?"

Donald did not stir. What was the source of the blood that pooled on the ground, that splattered the napkin? Cole searched for a wound. Maybe it was a head, or neck, or sucking chest wound. Touching Donald gently, Cole tugged Donald's shirt open, exposing his torso, then his arms and legs. Cole examined him thoroughly but found no wound. It had to be internal bleeding, flowing from his mouth. As long as his heart pumped, and he breathed, CPR was a no go. It would do more harm than good.

Cole needed to keep the man warm. Cole wore only a thin jacket that wouldn't provide enough warmth. Cole dropped Marco's leash and ran to the pavilion's kitchen area. Rummaging in the cupboards beneath the counter, he found a stack of white linen tablecloths. Running back, he rolled Donald onto his side, cradled his head under bunched fabric, and covered him. Cole tucked more of the cloths completely around Donald's torso.

Cole looked up to find Marco dragging his leash, slowly circling Donald and the table. The dog growled, lifted his head and sniffed. Each nostril moved independently, in different directions, like a chameleon's swiveling eyes. He sniffed again, as if testing every molecule of air. He lowered his head to the ground and huffed. As he moved around Donald's outstretched form, he paused every few inches and huffed up a lungful of scent from the sand. Certainly, he was gathering every clue he could.

The dog sat down and looked at Cole, expecting him to take charge, to do something. But what? Cole used to be a take charge kind of guy, but not anymore. Christine had died on his watch. Despite his being in charge, or perhaps because of it, he'd been unable to save her. He shuddered and returned to the task at hand.

Cole took his phone from his pocket, and turned on the time, date, and location feature. He snapped pictures of everything. Donald, the napkin, the table, the chairs, the coffee pot, and the cups. He did another round, moving in for close-ups of the man's face, his hands, and the soles of his shoes. He captured minute details, even blades of grass and impressions in the sand. He could be overreacting, but he documented everything, no matter how trivial. Just in case. As he had learned to do during his short rotation on shore patrol. At least taking photos could do no harm.

Marco dogged Cole's heels, watching everything he did with intense concentration. Marco continued to huff up the scents of everything Cole photographed.

Cole ran out of shots to take. He picked up Marco's leash and stepped back, removing them both once again from the scene. He hoped to hell the EMTs would arrive before Donald died.

Marco lifted his head and pricked up his ears. He looked toward the house, away from the river. No sirens alerted Cole to the ambulance's approach. Doors slammed and two men carrying equipment ran toward them. Beach grass and sand slowed their progress. Ordering Cole to back away, they did what EMTs do to stabilize a patient for transport. While they worked, they quizzed Cole about what had happened. Since he didn't know, Cole gave them an account of what he'd found, when he'd found it, and what he'd done to render aid. They worked quickly and efficiently, while Cole stood by like a voyeur at a crash scene. They lay Donald on a stretcher, loaded it into the back of the aid car and sped away, sirens receding into the distance.

Another death ensnared him. Cole walked to the river's edge, where water lurched in discordant waves, as if the tide were flooding and ebbing at the same time. The ground seemed to shift and swirl as though an earthquake had just struck. He sat down hard on the sand, his mind reeling.

* * *

I'd found the best pilot in the region. Ex-military who knew how to put the chopper down in the smallest possible spot in the worst conditions the country could throw at us. Not that that was the plan, but just in case. She came through as I'd hoped. Set us down without a hitch beside the most remote class-four river on the planet. Well, at least it was the most remote technical river run where I could get a permit to lead my adventure travel expedition. Challenging, but not too dangerous. Or so I thought.

"Cole." The pilot's voice came over my headset loud and clear as she pointed to our landing site. "Down there. Whadaya think?"

"Perfect." I gave her a thumbs up.

She landed the six of us and all our gear – tents, kayaks, helmets, paddles, freeze-dried food, personal water filters, not even one change of clothes, just extra socks and silk long-johns - safely. We had to travel light; we'd be spending five days on the river before we'd reach the next site where the chopper could land.

After we unloaded and watched the chopper take off, I got tents set up and dinner made before the light faded. We sat around the small campfire while I gave the group a thorough orientation. Then Christine went over the next day's plan. We'd tackle the first stretch of the river at dawn, then pull out to scout the next set of rapids. She always had a way of keeping it light, so everyone could relax and enjoy a good night's sleep. But I knew tomorrow's afternoon run could be a bear. We all said good night and disappeared into our tents.

Your old sports coach may have chided you to forgo sex the night before the big game, but Christine and I dismissed that as an old wives' tale. In fact, we excelled at making sweet love when we led our trips into the wild. There was no better preparation. Priming the pump, we called it.

Next morning the first stretch was easier than we'd thought. The group was stoked when we all pulled out at a gentle eddy with a small sandy beach. Everyone ate their snacks – some nuts and dried fruit – sipped some water and swapped some tall tales. We'd all been on wild rivers before, and I'd selected an experienced bunch.

All six of us scouted downstream. Clambering over boulders and loose shale, I found a rocky ledge and examined the rapids that lay ahead. I looked through the binoculars; I read the movement of the water. It was just too dangerous. I announced my disappointing news to the group – we'd have to portage our boats and gear downstream until we found a safe spot to relaunch and continue our journey.

Crestfallen that our first day out involved a long hike instead of an exhilarating run, we walked back to our little beach. All the way back Chris tried to change my mind, but I was clear – it was just too risky for me to let anyone paddle further. Christine kept up the fight, which got more heated by the moment. Our voices rose. Arguing in front of our clients was not going to help the situation. We stepped aside so the others could pass and return to our take-out spot.

She admitted that it was a highly technical run and that some among our group might not be up to the challenge. "Why don't you lead the hike downriver and I'll take my boat and scout this section? Then next year we'll know the best route through these rapids."

Seemed like a reasonable suggestion. She was the best river runner I knew. Better than me. But I had to stay with the group, and it was a very bad idea for her to go alone. I said so. She wouldn't budge.

When we arrived back at our boats, Christine launched and jumped in, fastening her spray skirt and donning her helmet. I yelled at her to stop. I ran, wading into the water to grab her boat, but she was already mid-stream.

"Okay, boys, I'll show you how it's done. I'm going for it. See you on the other side." She paddled hard past the boulders and out of sight. I never saw her again.

* * *

Marco crawled into Cole's lap. Pushing his nose under Cole's fingers, he invited Cole to caress his head. He licked Cole's hand.

Marco Diary Entry 6

Cole and I are running. Running fast, the way I like. Every day we take this path that leads from our house up into the park at the top of the hill. We usually run in the early morning but not today. This morning we went out to that big house and found that man on the beach. Now we are way off our schedule.

Even though Cole has longer legs than I do, I can keep up. He only has two legs and I have four. The truth is he's not as fast as I am. We run past the Rose Garden, the tennis courts, and up into the forest. I smell the prey, but Cole keeps me on leash, so I can't chase it. It doesn't really matter, because Cole never brings down rabbit and deer I flush, even though that's the alpha's job. It's like he doesn't know how to hunt at all. But even without prey, the hunt is exhilarating. We keep running on our trail in a big loop, and then home.

Back at the house, Cole goes into his gym across the house from his bedroom. He lifts weights, grunting as he adds heavy black discs to the long bar. I lick mud from my feet. I wait patiently but think about what I smelled and saw on the beach. It made Cole very sad. I wish I could tell Cole what I found out.

When he finishes, he is sweaty from his workout, so he takes a shower, then lies down on his bed and stares out the skylight. I lick his face because I know he's sad. He usually likes that, but not today.

I sit up and stare at the closed bedroom door, reminding Cole it's time for me to head to the kitchen. Nicholas always cooks dinner at this hour and I have to help. I try to be patient with Cole today, but he must know what time it is, he wears a watch.

I jump down from the bed and run to the door. I look back over my shoulder, but Cole's eyes are closed. I bark, as if there are demons approaching. That usually gets his attention. He opens his eyes, rolls over to stand, and opens the door for me. I dart down the stairs and out my dog door to the communal kitchen that sits at the center of the compound among everyone's houses.

Nicholas is alone in the kitchen, chopping vegetables. I lie down on one of my beds, this one under the counter where I have a good view of what the chef drops on the floor. He drops a piece of carrot and I scramble over to snatch it up. Then I return to my spot. That way, I clean the floor, so Nicholas doesn't have to. I stay out of his way and I get my treats. It's a good system. I invented it myself.

Shannon comes in, walking and talking fast at the same time as she always does. She sweeps me into her arms and kisses my head. Sometimes I don't like the way she manhandles me, forgetting that I am a full-grown male. But today it's okay.

"So, what the hell happened?" She sits down on one of the long wooden benches that surround the table.

"Not sure." Nicholas tosses vegetables into a baking dish and slides it into the oven next to the roasting chicken. "Cole says Bloomfield's in ICU. They're running tests, but don't know what happened yet."

"Where's Cole?"

Nicholas shrugs, but cocks his head to one side, indicating Cole's house.

"Damn." Shannon looks like she's about to growl. "Cole was finally making some progress since this little guy came along." She hugs me. "I mean agreeing to help Elena was a big step for him."

"Sure was. And he just doesn't need this shit."

"Maybe he needs . . ." she stops speaking and shudders. "Since you called, I've been checking around. Bloomfield has a stellar reputation, a man of the people, great guy. Funny, and fun to be around. Generous with his cohorts. All that. But there are fissures in the story. Some say on the down low that he's not so nice. Those folks won't say more. No details. It's kinda weird, the way they go silent. Like they're afraid of him."

Nicholas grunts. He takes a big wooden salad bowl from the shelf. "We can't worry about Bloomfield. It's Elena needs our help."

Shannon nods.

I jump down to clean the floor while Nicholas finishes making dinner and setting the table.

Elena sidles in, grabs a beer and sits down. She props her head in her hands, hiding her face. I get on my hind legs and put a paw on her knee. She needs to know I am here to help.

Nicholas puts a platter of dried figs filled with goat cheese on the table. I love figs, but they won't let me have cheese, so I am glad to see that he left a few figs unfilled for me. This is good, but I am ready for the meat course.

Cole walks through the door, pauses and looks around the room. "That's what I need." He gets himself a beer and sits next to Elena.

"Sorry I didn't find out anything about Javier today."

"I figured." Elena reaches down and pets my head. I'm a comfort to her, but not enough.

Nicholas walks back over to the stove and takes the chicken from the oven. Oh boy. My favorite. I jump up beside Shannon again and wag my tail. Nicholas carries the bird to the table and waits. To rest, he says. I don't know why a dead bird needs to rest before we eat it, but Nicholas always does it.

"Listen brother. . ." Nicholas often calls Cole his brother even though they are not from the same litter. I can tell by the way they look and smell. "You gotta take a step back here. You've been through enough."

Cole stands, picks up a knife and carves the bird. He puts some meat, figs, and a few roasted potatoes on a little plate, which he hands to Shannon. She puts it at my place. I have to wait until Cole tells me it's okay to eat. I start drooling. It's embarrassing, but I can't help it.

"I need to do just the opposite." Cole turns to Elena. "I'll go back tomorrow and find out where your brother is." He looks at me and nods. "Okay."

I eat fast, but even while I'm eating, I'm still listening. I hope he takes me with him. I tried to show him he missed a lot today. I don't blame him. People can't smell what I can. It's not their fault. But I smelled something really bad out there. Something on the table and near where the man fell. Not the blood. I know that smell. Something else. Something worse.

Chapter Six

Marco and Cole had no problem at the gate this time. Someone buzzed them in right away, even though the family could not possibly be happy to see them. After all, the day before Cole had been the harbinger of bad news. The aid car had come and gone through the service entrance, and by the time Cole and Marco had walked back to the house, the family was on their way out. They'd driven off in a black Hummer with tinted windows.

Needless to say, Cole was surprised when Portia met him at the door with no apparent hard feelings. "Good day, Mr. Steele." She frowned, lulling Cole into a false sense of normality. At least she did not wear the artificially chipper demeanor she'd had every other time Cole had encountered her. She greeted Marco, calling him "little one." He seemed not to like it.

She led them to a small dining area off the kitchen. A round table for six sat in a windowed alcove, a breakfast nook Cole supposed you'd call it. Papers lay strewn across the table, and her brother-in-law, Blake, pawed through them. He muttered, clutched his head, and seemed to be going mad with frustration. Marco watched him.

He finally spoke. "Where the hell is it?"

"Blake." Portia spoke sharply, almost shouting, as if to someone nearly deaf. Then she lowered her voice. "We have a guest."

Blake stared at Cole, eyes wild.

"Please sit, Mr. Steele." Portia pulled out a chair that was free of piled papers. "We were hoping you'd stop by."

They were? "What can I do for you?" Cole mimicked the words she'd spoken the day before but declined the chair. He didn't want Portia looming over him. Marco sat down beside Cole and looked out the window.

"We're hoping you'll keep yesterday's incident to yourself." She sidled further into the alcove until the sun streamed in behind her head, making her face unreadable.

"I'm not a gossip, if that worries you." Who would Cole tell? Who did he know that would even be interested?

"As you know, my father is a well-known and important man in our community." She tilted her head to the right so that the sun remained in Cole's eyes.

"Certainly." This was no time to quibble. As far as Cole knew Donald was just a rich white guy with inherited wealth from one of the timber baron families. A 'trustafarian' he and his friends called them in college. Not exactly a celebrity. "How's your father doing?"

"He's still in a coma." Her tone was lighthearted, in contrast to her words.

"Sorry to hear that." It felt ghoulish asking about the cause of his illness, and Cole really wanted to get on with the reason he'd come without seeming callous. How to broach the subject? Portia answered for him.

"So nice of you to come by, Mr. Steele." She circled the table, slid up beside Cole and took him by the elbow. Then, gently tugging, she started toward the door. Marco growled, but softly.

"Have either of you heard from Javier Ortega?" Cole stayed put.

Blake looked up at Cole, and for the first time the man paid attention to the conversation. Portia stared. A couple of seconds passed.

"Who?" Portia smiled, one of her pleasant smiles.

"Your head gardener." Cole hesitated to say more, curious to hear how they might respond.

"Oh," Portia waved her hand. "We know nothing about the staff. You'll have to ask . . ." She looked at Blake. "With whom should Mr. Steele speak?"

"Hmm." Apparently, Blake had to think about it. "Charley? That's right. Charley Hawkins. He handles all the personnel issues."

"Ah." Portia began tugging Cole's arm again. "His office is in the barn. Out on the farm."

Marco headed for the back door, pulling on his leash.

Portia opened the door and pointed. "Go out past the patio, then to your right, through the strawberries. You'll see the barn." She barely waited for them to step through the door before she closed it. The lock clicked into place.

Marco bounded ahead of Cole as they made their way across the expansive lawn, through the poplars, then a gate in the split rail fence, and into the strawberry patch. Marco stopped to sample the fruit. He liked it, and as they walked along the rows, he grabbed one every time he got the chance. Cole hoped the berries were organically-grown.

Gravel crunched beneath Cole's feet. This farm used to host "you-pick" shares to a select few from Portland. A kind of fruit club that Christine and Cole were never invited to join. They had come out to other farms – those open to the public – through different fruit seasons. Always fun excursions. He stopped. Here they were again, the flood of memories he'd struggled to banish.

Marco nudged Cole in the back of his calf, and Cole bent over to scratch behind his ears. The dog led the way from the strawberry patch, heading straight for the barn, as though following Portia's directions perfectly. How big was his vocabulary anyway? Large doors along the front made the barn look like it had once housed livestock, but inside Cole found conveyer belts and packing stations.

Six workmen packed asparagus and strawberries into clear plastic containers for sale. Two others laid the packages into large cardboard boxes, then loaded these into waiting panel trucks. Meanwhile six women continued to bring the produce in from the berry patches and asparagus fields. Marco pulled on his leash, trying to greet all the workers. Cole held him back. They were clearly busy.

The original barn had been tall and narrow, but lean-tos had been added to both sides. A hand-written sign, reading "office" hung on the door to the left-hand lean-to. None of the workers even looked up, so Cole and Marco walked to the door and knocked. No answer. Cole cracked the door open and looked in.

An enormous man with long white hair and beard sat behind the desk. He could have passed for Santa Claus but for his grimy Carhartt coveralls. A half empty bottle of bourbon sat beside an empty shot glass within easy reach.

"Yeah." He looked up with rheumy eyes.

"Sorry to disturb you. I'm Coleman Steele." Cole walked toward him with his hand extended.

"And?" The man didn't move.

"Portia sent me down to see you. You're Charley Hawkins, right?"

The man nodded. "Really?" He shuffled through a pile of papers. He sure wasn't going to put himself out for Cole, even when he mentioned the boss. Then again, maybe Portia wasn't his boss.

"I'm looking for Javier Ortega." Cole waited for some reaction.

"You and me both." He paused, looking at Cole as though they were done. "Haven't seen him in a few days."

"That's not surprising." Cole pulled over a stool that sat off to the side and sat beside the desk. Marco sat down beside Cole.

"Why's that?" Hawkins finally put down the papers he'd been looking through.

"His sister told me he was fired last week."

Charley sat up. Cole had finally said something that interested him. "First I've heard of it." He grunted.

"Blake said you handle all the personnel." Cole cocked his head to the side and squinted, trying to make sense of the inexplicable.

"Did he?" Hawkins started to stand but leaned forward and poured himself a shot instead. "I'm in charge of the farm-hands. The rest of the outdoor staff, security, that's all Javier's department. I don't have anything to do with the gardens, or the gardeners." His tone of voice told Cole he resented that.

"He's in charge of the gardeners too?" Why had Portia and Blake lied about this? It made no sense.

"Yep." Charley sipped his drink.

"Then who was Javier's boss?"

"Mr. Bloomfield." Charley stood and made his way around his desk. His girth made it nearly impossible in the cramped space. He stopped for a minute and towered over Cole and Marco. "Let's take a walk."

Cole let him pass before he stood. Marco jumped up, ready to get back outside. They followed the man out the wide barn doors to the graveled apron where the produce delivery trucks sat.

"Hey, Tony." Charley called to the man loading the boxed asparagus. "You're pretty tight with Javier, right?'

Tony finished loading a box, then took his time to straighten the stack before turning to face his boss. "Yeah, I guess."

"Seen him lately?"

Tony pulled his ball cap lower and shook his head. He went back inside for another box.

"I got a feeling that's not so." Charley grunted.

Marco followed Tony as he came back out of the barn. He sniffed the man's leg, keeping his nose planted against Tony's calf as he loaded the box into the truck.

"Elena's scared to death." Cole stepped forward to block Tony's retreat into the barn. "I told her I'd find Javier."

Tony looked at Cole, Charley, and then squatted to let Marco sniff his hands. He sat on his haunches, petting Marco's head. He took a pack of cigarettes from his shirt pocket, tapped one out, and lit up.

Charley grimaced and pointed to a prominent "No Smoking" sign posted on the side of the barn.

Tony looked away, stood and pulled a cell phone from his pocket. "I don't know where he is." He handed the phone to Cole. "But I found this in the garden yesterday afternoon. It's Javier's."

Marco Diary Entry 7

I get on my hind legs and sniff the phone Tony hands to Cole. There's a scent on it that reminds me of Elena. In fact, Tony smells a lot like Elena. I sniff his legs more carefully. I want to follow the phone's scent to the garden, but since Tony carried the phone in his pocket, I can't. The cigarette smoke gets in my nose. I sneeze and drop my feet to the ground.

We need to find the spot where Tony found the phone, but Cole doesn't say so to Tony. Instead he thanks the two men and asks where he can find the other gardeners. They exchange glances before telling Cole that the others haven't been in for a week.

Cole walks back toward the estate grounds where his car is parked. I am reluctant to go, hoping he'll check out the scent trails in the garden. Maybe he doesn't realize how much I could find out for him. People rarely think with their noses.

As he walks, he calls Elena to get Javier's address, and then asks her to meet us there. It's not as good a lead as mine, but it's still a good idea.

Chapter Seven

It would take Elena awhile to get to Javier's, so Cole took his time getting back to the car, Marco pulling on the leash, fighting to go upstream past the house. Eventually Cole let him have his head. Bounding eagerly, he dragged Cole through the dense stand of poplars that separated the working farm from the formal gardens of the estate. Lush grounds filled with neatly manicured lawns, perennial borders, discreetly camouflaged potting and equipment storage sheds. All very formal and well-managed, but slightly neglected, as though no one had worked here in days. Cole noted the aesthetic preference that Javier shared with Elena. It stretched her boundaries to adopt the naturalistic style for Cole's garden.

Marco, nose to the ground, yanked Cole this way and that, but he couldn't tell what the dog wanted. Was he after squirrel or something more significant? Cole had no way to tell. Cole followed, hoping Marco might lead him to Javier, or if not, to a clue to where he'd gone. But Cole saw nothing of significance, and Marco did not linger.

Hooking Marco's leash to his belt, Cole took Javier's phone from his shirt pocket and turned it on. It opened to a screen that asked for a password. At least the battery still held a charge. How long did a phone battery last? How long had that phone laid in the grass unnoticed?

Marco pulled Cole down one path, reversed course, and headed down another. Clearly searching rather than chasing prey. Cole let him lead. Curving around a froth of variegated shrubbery they ran into the security guard, Ordway. Marco stopped, ears pricked forward. Alert. He sat down and did not approach the man.

Cole expected another unpleasant confrontation, but Ordway surprised him.

"Hey." The guard walked toward Cole. "Thanks for taking care of Mr. Bloomfield."

"Of course." Cole nodded. "Have you seen Javier around? I understand he's your boss."

Ordway snorted. "Not much of a boss, if you ask me. But no, haven't seen him in a couple of days."

"When did you last see him?"

Ordway tipped his head back, squinting at the sky. "About five days ago."

"Odd. Did you tell anyone he was missing?"

"Who would I tell?" Ordway shrugged. "He worked directly under Bloomfield. I figured he knew about it. And then yesterday . . . you know."

"What do I know?" Cole asked

"How could I tell Mr. Bloomfield yesterday?"

That seemed reasonable. "You're head of security, aren't you?"

Ordway glared at Cole. One of those hard stares meant to intimidate. Cole almost laughed. It looked like the guard had learned it watching television. Cole had seen worse. Commanding officers who'd perfected the stare at sea, for instance. Ordway turned to walk away.

"Is it your job to monitor the security cameras? Open the gate when visitors arrive?"

Ordway looked back at Cole over his shoulder. "None of your goddamned business."

So much for the new friendly attitude. But he had Cole there; it was none of his goddamned business. Cole walked on with Marco to the car. They left without seeing anyone in the family and headed to Javier's house in Scappoose to meet Elena. Cole drove down and across the island to the bridge that led back to the mainland. He turned north on Highway 30. Elena had given Cole directions to Javier's mobile "tiny house", up a canyon west of the small town along the river. It took Cole longer to get there than he expected.

Although the house sat on wheels instead of a foundation, it looked like a small rustic cabin, surrounded by towering Western red cedar and Douglas fir. At only eight feet wide, its narrow interior was cramped but efficient. Elena sat at a small fold-out table methodically going through papers. She looked up as Marco and Cole came through the door.

"Just bills." She shrugged. Her eyes were red, and she'd clearly not had much sleep.

"Does he have a computer?" Cole glanced around. The whole place as tidy as Javier's gardens. The same aesthetic extended to his home.

"I'm sure he does." She began to rummage through the small cupboards along the wall beneath the table. When she didn't find one, they searched other compartments throughout the house. Under the stairs to the loft, in the tiny kitchen, even in the bath. No luck. Elena climbed the stairs and searched under the bed, then in the compartments under the eaves. Nothing.

"That's really strange." She looked at Cole.

Cole handed her Javier's phone. "It's password protected."

"I can probably figure that out." She sat again. The dark wings of her brows drew together. "Ah. I know." She tapped the screen and sat back. She opened the phone app and looked at the call log. There were a few incoming missed calls from her over the past few days, including one from yesterday. All the outgoing calls were several days old, and none were more recent than five days ago. One, to a Portland area code, lasted only a minute. Another, lasting three minutes, had been made to a blocked number. The last one was to Elena's cell.

"That has to be the one when he told me he'd been fired and was on his way over."

She checked the text messages. Same story. Texts from Elena. But yesterday Javier had received a text from Bloomfield. "See me now." It'd come in at six in the morning. Odd, since Javier had already been fired and Elena believed he was already missing.

Elena then deduced the password for his voice mail. Two messages from Elena asking him to call her. Then one message from a man who did not identify himself. "You better get over here. Shit's about to hit the fan." They'd been sorted from most recent to oldest.

"That's Tony." Elena wrinkled her brow, reflecting her distaste at hearing his voice. "I knew there'd be trouble as soon as he got involved." Things between them must have been worse than Cole thought.

The three-minute outgoing call had been made five minutes after Tony's call. Both were from five days ago.

"Guess I better go back and talk to Tony," Cole said.

Elena hunched over and put her head in her hands. "I really hoped we'd find something."

Cole patted her back. "Me too."

Marco pulled Cole toward the door. He followed the dog outside, where he began to huff up scents from the ground. He led Cole to the back of the house. Elena suddenly flew out the door, ran by them, and crawled under the house. Marco crawled under with her, pulling to the end of his leash. Cole knelt to watch them. Elena turned over on her back and pulled something from the underside of the house. She squirmed her way out with a laptop computer tucked under her arm.

"I'd forgotten about that compartment." Elena blinked her eyes. "He'd sketched it on the early building plans."

Marco crawled out and shook himself. Cole had noticed on previous occasions that as much as Marco liked to roll on the ground, he didn't like twigs and dirt and leaves sticking to his hair. He ran to Elena and sniffed the computer thoroughly. There seemed to be an abundance of tantalizing scents on it.

Elena went back inside and sat again at the tiny table. She didn't explain why Javier would keep his laptop under his house, nor why he had a hidden compartment in the first place.

For the moment it felt smarter not to ask.

She booted it up, using the same password as she had on the phone. She checked his contact list in his email program. The blocked number from the phone – the call that had lasted three minutes - did not appear here either. She looked through his emails, and found notes from herself, and their brother, Tony, and the farm manager, Charley

"Does your brother, Tony, work for Bloomfield too?"

Elena nodded. "That's what I heard from Javier."

"At the farm?"

She nodded again. "But not in the gardens."

"Why didn't you tell me?"

Elena leaned back and sighed. "Javier told me Mr. Bloomfield is very secretive. Didn't want anyone 'spying' on him." She used air quotes around the word, spying. "No one who works for him is allowed to talk about it."

"Why?"

She shrugged.

"But I knew about Javier."

"Only because I told you." She began to cry. "I thought maybe that's why he was fired."

"That's ridiculous." Now Cole felt really bad. He touched her shoulder. Marco climbed up into her lap. She took him in her arms and hugged him tight.

Could this explain Portia's and Blake's, and even Charley's, weird behavior about Javier and personnel matters? Maybe, but it didn't explain why Bloomfield was so secretive. Feeling awkward, Cole turned back to Javier's computer. The emails seemed innocuous. Work related messages from Charley. Plans to meet up after work for a beer or two from Tony. Nothing raised any red flags. Cole turned to his browsing history.

He found link after link to news stories by the same reporter about small local companies that had gone out of business. There must have been six or seven articles, ranging from stories about a consulting firm that set up private internet and email servers, to horticultural companies, to a small private security firm with the same name Cole had seen on Ordway's badge. None of it seemed to require hiding the computer under the house.

"How about we take this back to the house and print out these articles? Maybe we'll figure out what drew Javier's interest." Cole began to close the lid as Elena stood.

"Wait." Elena reached over and clicked on one more article.

It was the reporter's obituary. He'd been killed in a car crash on a back road off highway 30. Just over the bridge from Sauvie Island.

Marco Diary Entry 8

I jump into Cole's car, ready for action. Anything Cole wants, I'm ready to do. I stick my head out the window, watching, making sure there's no suspicious activity, and wondering where we're going next. Cole speeds up and my ears flap in the wind. Now this is fun. I think Cole and Elena – who is following us in her car - should stick their heads out the window too. Everyone is too sad. I know we have serious business to do, but we all need moments of joy.

We return to the compound. Cole and Elena make a beeline for the kitchen, while I do a quick perimeter check and deposit some markers along the property line. Security is lax around here, and even though I try to show Cole how to take care of it, he never pees in the yard. I'll keep trying; I think he'll get it eventually. He's pretty smart for a human.

It's close to my lunchtime, so I run to the kitchen and get to work cleaning up the floor. The meal is nearly ready, and I jump up to my place at the table. I smell several courses, including a quinoa and roasted golden beet dish that is one of my favorites. There's also poached salmon with hollandaise and a strawberry tart. Nicholas is good at what he does.

Shannon isn't home yet so her lap is not available, and I sit quietly at my place. I want to hear everything Elena and Cole have to say. There's a nook in the kitchen with a computer and printer where Nicholas writes his cook books, researches menus, and orders food for all of us. He always talks aloud when he's working.

Cole plugs in Javier's phone, puts Javier's computer on the desk, plugs it into the printer, and starts printing page after page while we eat. I am glad no one discusses our investigation during the meal. I don't like distractions while I'm eating. It's uncivilized.

After the last bite of tart, after everyone has enjoyed the food and thanked Nicholas – I give him a quick lick when he collects my plate – Cole and Elena read the articles and pass them to each other. I search under the table for any scraps that may have fallen while Nicholas does the dishes.

Cole leans back and waits for Elena to finish the last article. "So, why did Javier save these articles?"

"I honestly don't know."

"He never said anything to you about this?" Cole gestures to the papers spread out on the table.

Elena looks down at her hands. "Look, I'm sorry I didn't tell you about Tony."

I jump up next to her and lick her fingers. She needs my attention. And she might have a treat in her hand.

"What's the story with Tony?" Cole crosses his arms.

Elena reaches out to me, burying her face in my hair.

Cole waits for an answer.

"He brings trouble wherever he goes. He was a bully when we were kids and he's a bully now. Takes advantage of everyone in the family." Her voice is muffled so she lets go of me and looks up. "I try to stay away from him."

"I'm sorry." Cole looks down and away. "Do you think he had anything to do with Javier's disappearance?"

Elena almost drops me. "No. I don't believe that."

"Why does Javier have a secret compartment under his house?" Now Cole looks ready to growl. "And how do you know about it?"

Elena presses her face into my fur again. "When Javier saw how secretive Mr. Bloomfield was, he started to wonder why. He snooped a bit. He never told me what he found." She stops speaking and looks up. I lick tears from her face. "I'd seen his house plans and guessed if he had something to hide it would be in that compartment. I forgot about it. But it's kinda weird. That compartment runs the whole length of his house, but his laptop was the only thing in there."

Cole nods and they're quiet for a while. "You should have told me all this when you asked for my help." Cole's voice is softer than usual. Sometimes he talks that way to me when I do something wrong. He goes very quiet.

Nicholas strides across the room and thumps Cole's shoulder. It makes a loud sound like drumming on a log. Like he's angry. But then he sits down with us. "What's the story?"

"Every one of these articles is about a small company that went out of business three years ago." Cole digs through the papers and hands some to Nicholas.

"A security firm, a horticulture supply company, and a cyber-security business." Nicholas lays the papers back down on the table and pours everyone fresh coffee, except for me. I like the way it smells, but I tried it once. It tastes terrible. "What's special about these three?"

Cole picks up one piece of paper. "This security firm was owned by Reggie Ordway, the security guard out at the estate." He puts that down and picks up another. "This one – a horticultural supply company – was owned by Charley Lawson, the guy in charge of farm operations at

Bloomfield's." He picks up the last. "The cyber-security company? Owned by Blake Blanchard, Donald's son-in-law."

There's a long silence. I think everyone is thinking very hard. I know I am.

"Well, that's interesting." Nicholas rocks back in his chair and grunts. "Shannon called earlier. She's looking through court filings in her spare time . . . not that she has much of that, but you know her. She got curious when people she checked with stopped talking, so she dug a little deeper." He pours everyone more coffee.

"And?" Cole pours a glug of cream into his coffee. Now **that** I like, but Cole doesn't allow me to have cream, so I don't even ask.

"She found some lawsuits filed against Bloomfield. Some pending. Some settled. The settlements are sealed." Nicholas blows on his coffee. I don't know why he does that.

"You think it has to do with these business closures?" Cole leans forward now.

"I'd bet my new sous vide cooker on it." He laughs. "But I'd be cheating you, my friend. There are two pending suits that aren't sealed. In one the plaintiffs are Charley Lawson and Tony Ortega. And guess who filed the other?"

"Reggie Ordway?" Cole laughs too.

"Nope. I shoulda made that bet." Nicholas shakes his head. "Blake Blanchard."

Chapter Eight

Cole slapped his hand on the table and stood. He had more energy than he'd had in a year. He picked up Javier's phone, gathered up the relevant articles along with the reporter's obituary, grabbed the pup's halter and leash, and headed for the door. Luckily, he'd reserved the share-car for the rest of the month. He and Marco piled into the car and took off once more for the Bloomfield estate.

Cole drove to the service entrance instead of the main gate. He found a length of chain wrapped around a post to keep the gate closed, but the padlock hasp was open. He'd figured the front entrance and its imposing security was all for show, and he was right.

Looking for Charley and Tony he drove to the barn. With Marco at his side, Cole walked into Charley's office without knocking, and sat again in the visitor's chair. Charley looked up and grunted. Cole wasn't sure where to start so he waited to see what Charley might volunteer. They stared at each other. Marco sat down beside Cole and looked back and forth between the two men. Cole let go of Marco's leash, walked to the door, and called to Tony to join them. Marco stayed put and Cole sat down again to wait.

Tony poked his head in the door. "Yeah?"

"Let's talk about your brother." Cole waved him in.

Tony and Charley exchanged looks, but neither spoke.

"Okay. How about this?" Cole took Javier's cell from his pocket, opened voice mail and played the message. "Better get over here. Shit's about to hit the fan." He hit the save button and put the phone back in his pocket.

Tony's shoulders slumped. He came all the way into the office and perched on a side table. The other two men eyed each other, and Cole waited.

"It's none of your concern." Charley quietly broke the silence.

"That ship has sailed." Cole turned to Tony. "Elena asked for my help and she's going to get it. Why pretend you barely know your own brother?"

Tony nodded. "Okay." He looked at Charley again, then looked back at Cole. "Didn't seem like any of your business." He stopped, shifting his butt on the table.

Cole pulled the article about Charley's company going out of business from his jacket pocket. "What happened?" He leaned over and slid the paper in front of Charley.

"Crap." Charley looked at it but didn't pick it up.

"And then the two of you came to work here and filed a lawsuit against your boss. What the hell is going on?" Cole waited some more, until Marco poked him in the knee.

Cole slammed his fist on the table. Both men jumped.

"Aw hell." Charley stood. "You don't scare me, jackass."

Cole leaned back. He was being a jackass, but Javier was still missing, and Elena was still frightened. "You're right. It's none of my business. But I'm going to keep digging. And I'm going to find Javier. I'd appreciate your help." He waved Charley into his seat, and the man sat again.

"Tell me about the shit hitting the fan." Cole turned to Tony.

Tony scooted back on the table until his feet dangled. "Mr. Bloomfield found out the three of us – me, Charley, and Javier - were planning to open our own business."

"And what? He thought that was disloyal? After putting Charley out of business in the first place?" Marco stood on his hind legs and put his front paws on Cole's thigh.

"Something like that." Charley said.

"Fill me in." Cole stroked Marco's head and he sat back down.

"The son of a bitch ruined me. I had nothing left." Charley's jaw tightened. "Then my wife got sick. Needed a big operation. The bastard offered me a job. Knew I couldn't refuse."

"And he wanted to take advantage of your expertise." Cole began to understand why no one talked about Donald. Afraid of retaliation if they told the truth.

"Take advantage. You got that right." Charley pushed the article Cole had put on his desk back toward him.

"So?" Cole gestured to the paper.

"I filed a lawsuit to recover the money he owed me. When I had my own business, he hired me to consult here. Bought a ton of my products for the farm and the gardens. Never paid. That's how he drove me out of business."

After that, why would Donald hire him, and why would he come to work here? And why wait three years to file suit to recover the money? Cole hoped this would start to make sense at some point, because it sure didn't yet. He craned his head around to look at Tony again. "How did you get involved?"

"I'd just bought into Charley's business. We were gonna be partners." Tony folded his arms across his chest.

"Did you already work here?"

Tony nodded. "Javier got me the job. He's tight with Bloomfield." He took an old-fashioned metal lighter from his shirt pocket, flipped the top open then closed, again and again.

"So, when Charley came to work here, you planned some kind of payback, I assume."

"Didn't know how we were gonna do it, but, by God, somehow, we were going to get him." Charley leaned forward, and glared at Tony, fidgeting with his cigarette lighter.

Cole thought some more about the shit hitting the fan. "You were skimming? Taking a little here, a little there?"

Charley just stared at Cole.

"Javier helping you?"

Tony slipped the lighter back into his pocket and leaned forward, propping his elbows on his thighs. "No. He wouldn't have anything to do with it. He convinced us to restart our company instead, but this time we'd grow cannabis. It's about to explode, you know. But he said it would be all three of us this time. He had a stash. A bankroll."

"Really?" Cole was surprised. "Where'd he get the money?"

"That was the beauty of it." Tony laughed. "He got it from Bloomfield."

"How?"

Tony shrugged.

Cole didn't push it. He'd come back to that when he had some leverage. "So how did the lawsuit come about?"

Charley looked away. "That was Blake's idea."

Marco Diary Entry 9

I am ready to get moving. Cole is talking to these men for too long. I want to go back to that little house without walls on the beach. I need to show Cole what I know about it, but he doesn't get my hints.

I trot beside him as his long strides move fast through the farm. We pass through a grove of tall trees until we get to grass and patches of flowers. I pull ahead, straining against my halter. I want to explore this part of the garden more. If only Cole will follow me. He does for a while, but a lot of the smells are weak now and I have to backtrack. I think he gets bored when I do that.

I smell a lot of different people on the garden path. The man in uniform who was mean to Cole when we first came, his scent is everywhere. So is the smell of the man who was in the kitchen pawing through papers. I smell all three of those women we met the first day, but their scents are weak. I stop and sniff three blades of grass for a long time, running my nose up and down each one. A woman's scent, but not one I have smelled before. I take off, running, to follow the scent, but I hit the end of my leash quickly.

I turn and look at Cole. He follows me as I lead him away from the main house and find a nearly overgrown path behind that terrible place on the beach. The path narrows and almost disappears. I smell the woman's scent as it weaves between shrubs.

Cole stumbles trying to follow me. After a while he whistles, gives my leash a quick tug, and heads toward the big house. I don't like it. I don't budge, hoping he'll take the hint. He frowns and points back toward the house. Discouraged, I trot after him until he climbs the stairs to the back patio. He knocks on a sliding glass door. I don't smell, or see, or hear anyone. I sit beside Cole to wait. After just a minute, he slides the door open and we step inside.

Chapter Nine

Cole stood just inside with Marco at his side. The dog's ears perked up on high alert. Odd that the door wasn't locked, but Cole would take any break he could get.

"Hello?" Cole kept his voice down. He didn't want to startle anyone. Yeah, right. He walked further into the house and turned toward the sunroom off the kitchen. Empty. No papers strewn about the table to snoop through. Too bad. He and Marco reversed course and padded along to the hallway towards the front door. A Persian runner muffled his footsteps and kept Marco's nails from clicking on the bare floor. Cole stopped to listen but heard nothing.

Marco's head lifted sharply, his ears pricked. He led Cole to the staircase.

"Hello? Anyone home?" Cole called out.

A door upstairs slammed shut. Marco barked. Cole glanced into the living room with its gaudy fireplace, the three gilt chairs still standing in a tight circle. No one.

Marco pulled Cole back to the hallway and to the foot of the stairs. Cole hesitated. It seemed beyond rude to go upstairs to hunt someone down. But polite behavior would get him nowhere, and civility hardly seemed the norm in this household. He and Marco climbed the stairs, pausing occasionally to call out and await a response. They reached a vast landing at the top of the stairs to find another living room with a bar along one wall and an enormous TV screen opposite. A red leather couch and two matching club chairs formed a seating area around a glass coffee table. This must be where the family actually gathered, not the nearly empty formal living room downstairs. But where had the furniture he'd seen last year at the party gone?

Two long hallways flanked the staircase on either side, forming an open gallery. Cole turned to look. Floor to ceiling paintings hung between each of the five closed doors on both walls. All were portraits of family members. One for each of the three daughters, one of a woman Cole had never seen, and six of Donald. Cole walked down one hall, passing five closed doors and five paintings, to the end. He turned and crossed to the other hallway, again passing five doors and five paintings, and came back to the head of the stairs. Had he stumbled into a Vegas brothel in the 1970s, before he was even born? He'd seen this kind of decor in movies, but thought it was fiction.

The paintings were embarrassing. In each of the four paintings of women, a woman was dressed either like child beauty queens or fashion models in the skimpiest of outfits. In one Krista sat in Donald's lap. Despite being an adult, she had dressed to look like Jon-Benet Ramsey, a child beauty queen who'd gone missing from her family home in 1990 and was found murdered some days later. Deeply disturbing.

In another, Cole saw defiance. A voluptuous woman, dressed in a silver chain-mail chemise that covered almost nothing, held up her middle finger. Cole did not recognize her. He was both horrified and mesmerized. He couldn't stop staring.

The portraits of Donald showed him bare-chested in six different power poses. In one he wore a jewel encrusted crown. In another he held an enormous gold sports trophy. In a third he posed with a rifle and one foot on the neck of a dead elephant. The portraits hinted at pornography and glorified the slaughter of wild animals. Appalling.

He took out his phone and started snapping pictures. They might be useful to pry information out of someone.

He sat down on the club chair that faced the staircase and the doorways. Marco jumped into his lap. They waited as patiently as possible. The longer he sat the more repulsed he became. His opinion of Donald sank lower than whale shit.

A half hour later Blake emerged from one of the doorways in the middle of the wall on the right-hand side of the gallery. That doorway was flanked by the portrait of Blake's wife, Brenda, on one side, and a portrait of bare-chested Donald sporting gold chains around his neck on the other.

Blake startled when he saw Cole, then walked quickly forward. Cole stayed seated, pondering Blake's repeated startle response. Did he have some kind of psychological disorder? These people seemed to respond to dominance behavior. Not rising to greet the son-in-law felt like the power play. Marco jumped down and sat beside Cole.

"Good afternoon." Cole nodded and pointed to the other club chair. "Have a seat."

Blake hesitated.

"We need to talk," Cole said.

Blake sat with his back to the stairs and the bizarre portrait gallery.

"As you know, I'm trying to find Javier Ortega. He is your father-in-law's head gardener." Cole waved a hand at Blake when he started to interrupt. "It's nonsense to pretend you don't know who he is. In my search for him I've uncovered a whole mess of family secrets."

Blake stiffened. He glanced over his shoulder.

Cole had scared him. "Donald put you out of business; and then you came to work here and married his daughter. And now you're suing him. What's the story?"

"You're wrong." Blake sat back, crossing his legs, relaxing into his chair.

Well, those particular secrets didn't frighten him.

"I was married to Brenda before he put me out of business." Blake shrugged. "After it happened, and I'd lost everything, he offered me a good job, so I took it. To get back on my feet."

"So why the lawsuit?"

Blake picked at his sock. "Pride." He offered a weak smile.

Cole leaned forward resting his forearms on his knees. "Did he use the same tactics with you that he used on Charley? Racking up a lot of debt and refusing to pay?"

Blake raised his eyebrows, then nodded. "Yes. And I wanted that money back."

"What changed? Why now?" Cole didn't expect an answer.

"What does any of this have to do with Javier?" Blake asked a good question.

"I don't know, honestly. But everything here is so strange. Everyone's behavior borders on the bizarre. I just can't believe there's no connection to his disappearance." Cole looked at the portrait of Brenda and shook his head. "I mean how can you tolerate this portrait of your wife?"

Blake looked back at the portrait and laughed. His eyes bugged. "What's the big deal? It pleases her dad. So what?"

"How in the world could that please any father?" Once again, Cole didn't expect him to answer, but he did.

"Donald loves to paint. It's his favorite hobby." Blake shrugged. "Outside of gardening that is."

"Donald painted these?" Cole's voice rose with the loathing he felt. It was so repellent he didn't know how to proceed. He got up to take a closer look. The setting was the beach pavilion. Brenda wore the skimpiest bikini he'd ever seen. It all just got creepier. Marco nudged Cole in the back of his knee as if to say – let's get out of here. Cole agreed. But he needed information that was actually useful.

Cole turned back to Blake, stepping close to the chair to tower over him. "Why did you encourage Charley and Tony to sue?"

Blake rocked back in his chair and looked up at Cole. "That was my mother-in-law's idea."

"Brenda's mother?" Cole stepped away, but Marco sat still. "I thought she was dead."

Marco Diary Entry 10

At last! Cole is walking, practically running, down a path that holds the scent of that unfamiliar woman. It isn't the path I found earlier. It's not overgrown, but not well-used either. The overgrown path goes to the beach. This path leads away from the big house into the forest, toward the road and away from the river.

The woman left her scent on the overgrown path a while ago but walked this path this morning. Now we're getting somewhere. I bark once to let Cole know, but he is in much too big a hurry to answer.

Chapter Ten

Cole felt propelled into some strange world where nothing was as it seemed. He followed Marco, who bounded down the narrow but well-traveled trail. His enthusiasm matched what he'd shown earlier on the overgrown path. Maybe he really was onto something, and not just chasing squirrels.

He pulled Cole to the door of a cottage that looked like a Helen Allingham painting. Art history was one of the few classes where Cole had paid attention, and his memory of nineteenth century English painters paid off occasionally. Paid off might be an exaggeration, but sometimes it helped him feel grounded. A small cottage-garden surrounded the house, and a forest of conifers and maples surrounded the garden. Very quiet and secluded.

Cole knocked on the door. A woman opened it immediately, as though anticipating his arrival. She smiled broadly. "Come in." She swept her arm back inviting Cole and Marco in.

Despite the gray hair, plaid skirt, and sturdy leather walking shoes, Cole recognized her immediately from her portrait. She was the one who gave the painter the finger. In person she had a round, smooth face and a ready smile.

"Mr. Steele." She pointed toward her small sitting room off the foyer. "Please join me for tea." She bent over and fondled Marco's ears. "Hello, precious child. You're welcome here."

Marco wagged his tail and licked her nose.

The room was crammed with overstuffed chairs covered in bold floral patterns. A small couch, with matching upholstery, sat at a right angle to the chairs. An old-fashioned mahogany coffee table stood in front of the sofa, displaying a large ceramic bowl, filled with fresh fruit, and a dozen coasters. Throw pillows in primary colors were tucked everywhere, exuberantly battling with the furniture for attention. Shelving lined the pale green walls, every shelf crowded with exquisite small sculptures and blown glass figurines.

"Please sit." She gestured to one of the chairs, then patted the sofa next to her as she sat. "Come here, little one."

As Marco approached, she unclipped his leash, and he jumped on the couch next to her.

Cole's eyebrows raised on their own. Marco seemed overly at ease with the woman.

"Blake tells me you're looking for Javier Ortega, Mr. Steele. How can I help?"

"Mrs. Bloomfield?" Cole stammered. This perfectly pleasant moment struck him as completely bizarre.

The woman shook her head. "Call me Irene," She shifted, pulling her skirt lower to cover her knees. "Although I am still married to . . ." she shuddered. ". . . that man, I have not used his name in years." She paused and looked at Cole intently. "As I said, how can I help?"

This threw Cole more than the obstruction he'd encountered earlier. He wasn't sure where to begin. "Do you know where Javier Ortega is?"

"No, of course not. I'd hardly keep track of the comings and goings of the hired help, would I?"

"Do you have any idea why he was fired?" Cole had planned to be less direct but going straight at it seemed the best approach.

"Of course not. You're not a good listener, are you?" Her exasperation was clear. "But I liked the boy. He was a good influence on that man." She wrinkled her nose when she spoke the last two words.

Apparently, she did keep track of Javier's comings and goings to some extent. "In what way?" Cole didn't know if his question was relevant, but he was genuinely interested.

She stared out the front bay window for a moment. "He seemed able to make the S.O.B. care about something other than himself." She paused. "At least, for a while."

"And what was it he cared about?"

"The garden. The farm." She waved her hand vaguely toward the river. "The environment. But it didn't last long, I guess. Because now Javier is gone." She stopped speaking and stared out the window, then shook herself. "Let's talk about something more enjoyable. You do know that asshat is in the hospital, don't you? Looks like he might not make it." She smiled.

Cole took a deep breath, taking time to figure out the best approach. Obviously, she appreciated getting to the heart of issues. "Can you tell me anything about the lawsuits Blake, Charley, and Tony have filed against your husband?"

She placed an index finger under her chin. "Why yes I can. But I prefer that you do not refer to him that way. I can't stand to be thought of as his wife. Those boys . . ." She pursed her lips. "Their silly lawyer told them not to talk about it, but I don't have to listen to that blowhard." She gave Cole a mischievous smile. "Where shall I begin?"

Cole started to respond, but she held up a finger – the index finger – and shushed him.

"I wasn't asking you." She tilted her head. "At the beginning, I think. Well, not quite." She wagged her finger at me. "I love my two daughters, but they are weak and need a lot of guidance."

"Don't you have three daughters?" Cole knew better than to butt in with a willing witness, but he needed clarity about the relationships. After all, twenty minutes ago he had not known of this woman's existence.

"Don't interrupt, dear." She frowned. "I do not count that despicable cow."

"Which one?" Cole blurted.

"You can't tell the difference? Are you implying that all three are despicable cows?"

"No. Not at all."

"Just teasing, dear." She patted Marco. "He's a silly man, your papa, isn't he?" She turned to face Cole again. "Portia, of course."

Cole kept his mouth shut.

"I got Blake and Brenda together. I wanted her to get away from here. He's a good husband and used to be a good provider. But he has no backbone. None at all. I thought he'd do a better job of protecting her. And I'd hoped he'd break that bastard." She lifted one shoulder in a half-hearted shrug. "Well, that's all behind us now. Krista – she's always been a mousy one. Knuckled under to the bastard's bullying from day one. And unfortunately, that's resulted in her having no judgment whatsoever about men. None at all. Chosen a boyfriend who's simply no good. A gold digger. Can't stand the man." She sounded like an aristocrat laying down the law on a BBC drama.

She bent over and took Marco's face in her hands. "What's your name, sweet one?"

"Marco," Cole answered, even though he wasn't sure he should.

She looked up and smiled. "Well, of course it is. He is a wanderer, after all."

How did she know he was a wanderer? Cole didn't ask. He knew better than to distract her. But his skin crawled when he pondered whether she, Blake, Ordway, or someone else had been spying on his household.

Obviously, she and Blake were in close communication. She'd known that Cole and Marco were on their way over. She knew he was looking for Javier. And Blake had just told Cole that she had urged him, Charley, and Tony to sue. Cole suddenly imagined her as the ring leader of a band of avengers. He shuddered.

"Krista and Brenda. Such sweet babies, such sweet women." She cocked her head to one side. "Brenda first. She's smart, and if that man had not interfered, she and Blake could have built something successful. They both understand cyber-security, hacking . . ." She fluttered her hand and chuckled. "Well, things I don't know anything about."

She paused for so long Cole wondered if she wanted him to say something. But he waited and made a mental note to ask Shannon to beef up their cyber-security.

"Would you care for a cup of tea, dear?" Without waiting for his answer, she picked up her cell phone and sent a text.

"That would be nice." The longer Cole stayed the more information he was likely to get.

"I funded their company, you know. So, when Donald forced them out of business, I lost quite a bit of money." The phone dinged a reply and she set it down again on the side table. "But not all of it, of course."

Cole called on every ounce of discipline to keep from blurting questions. Where did her money come from? Why didn't she divorce Donald if she hated him so much? Why did she stay here? And most disturbing of all, why did she allow Donald to paint those portraits? Did she condone what they implied? It didn't seem likely, given the motif of her portrait. None of those questions would help him find Javier, so he kept his mouth shut.

"Krista is another matter. She doesn't have much in the way of brains. I was looking for a suitable mate for her, but she fell in love with a real jackass." She used air quotes around "fell in love."

She talked as if a marriage was more financial merger than an affair of the heart. Is that what she believed? Maybe that's why she had married Donald in the first place.

"I am trying to put a stop to her foolishness, but so far I have failed." She leaned back and sighed, inviting Marco into her lap.

Cole didn't like their chumminess. He'd thought Marco a better judge of character.

"How do the lawsuits fit in?" Cole's question broke the silence that had fallen.

She looked at him sharply, as if coming out of a reverie. "Oh, they don't." She waved her hand, dismissing his question. "I just wanted to see that prick squirm. I knew it would drive him crazy. He hates to lose, and he thinks everyone is scared to death of him."

She stopped when a frumpy woman about her own age entered carrying a tea tray, which she set on the coffee table.

"Thank you, Jackie." Irene smiled up at her.

Jackie wore traditional maid's attire. A crisp white apron with a lacey bodice over a black dress. She even wore a white cap over her iron gray hair. She was plump and pleasant-looking with weathered skin and piercing gray eyes.

"Think nothing of it." Jackie also smiled and wagged her finger. "But don't spoil your appetite, Irene. I have a special supper planned."

She turned and bowed toward Cole. "Mr. Steele." She left the room.

Irene scooted forward on the sofa. "Shall I be mother?" She picked up the tea pot and poured each of them a cup. Handing the cup and saucer to Cole with one hand, she lifted a plate of cookies from the tray with the other and offered some to him. "Biscuits?"

Marco perked his ears and wagged his tail.

Cole accepted the cup and chose a cookie from the plate she offered. Another plate on the tray held a selection of dog biscuits.

Irene settled again. Gesturing toward the doorway to the hall, she said, "Jackie is an old friend. She loves dogs."

Cole felt increasingly unbalanced. He sipped his tea, hoping to regain equilibrium. "I'm trying to understand why Blake and Charley and Tony would come to work for Donald after his shabby treatment of them."

Irene held up her index finger, shushing him again. Then she picked up a treat for Marco, who took it carefully from her fingers. He wagged some more. "We'll get to that." She frowned. "Where was I? In short, my daughters need all the help they can get. And they will get it from me. Come hell or high water. Keeping that cocksucker off kilter is one way to go."

Then why did she allow them to sit for those portraits? The question wouldn't turn loose of Cole but asking it would not help. So, he asked one that could be relevant.

"Why did Donald hire them? There are plenty of other experienced farm managers."

"That one's easy, dear. That man loves nothing more than keeping people under his thumb and squashing them like bugs when the time is right."

"So, you encouraged the lawsuits as some sort of payback?"

She sipped her tea and nibbled on a cookie. "Not exactly." She handed Marco another treat. "It's a more long-term strategy." She did not explain further.

Cole waited, his patience wearing thin. "To accomplish?" He hoped she'd fill in the blank.

"Why, to bring about his financial ruin, of course." She laughed. A self-satisfied chuckle.

Someone pounded on the front door. Whoever had knocked didn't wait. The door flew open. Blake burst into the room.

"It's Donald." He shouted. He drew a deep breath. "He's awake."

Marco Diary Entry 11

Cole drives really fast. Faster than usual. He's weaving in and out of traffic, around trucks and out from behind slow-moving cars. I'm getting thrown around, so I brace myself every time he swerves. He finally notices and drives more carefully.

He parks the car in its usual place – a block uphill from our house – and jumps out. He doesn't even hook up my leash. That's not like him. But it's okay. I know the way to our gate and I run to it. I get there before he does.

He opens the gate and dashes to the potting shed. He stops. Elena's not there. He writes a note and leaves it on the potting bench, then leans down and takes my face in his hands. "Gotta go out for awhile. I won't be long." He caresses my head and gives me a treat, then runs back through the gate and down the street away from the car.

I am disappointed he doesn't take me with him, but I know my duty as chief of security. I wonder where everyone else is. I check the kitchen, squeezing through my dog door. I must be gaining weight. I bet Nicholas will put me on a diet when he notices. I don't think that's fair, given how big he and Shannon are. They eat way more food than I do.

No one's in the kitchen. I trot over to Elena's little cottage near the vegetable garden. It's very quiet. I nudge the front door with my nose and bark, but she doesn't open it.

If everyone's out, I am in charge. I need to be extra vigilant. I do a slow, careful perimeter check. I examine every possible point of entry, taking my time to double-check every fence post, every shrub and tree and flower that grows near the fence line. Nothing is out of place. And everything smells as it should.

As I head to Nicholas and Shannon's place at the back, I smell a snake. It slithers through the grass and under the garden shed. I go after it. I see its tail disappear just as I get there. I start digging. As fast as I can. I'm a very good digger. The best. I dig fast and deep. I keep digging until the front half of my body fits down the hole. I'm hoping to catch it if I go deep enough.

"Hey." Elena shouts at me.

I keep digging. She'll thank me as soon as she sees what I'm doing. Once I sink my teeth into that reptile. But she yells again and pulls me up out of the hole.

"No. No. No," she shouts.

I don't know why. I'm a good hunter and could have solved a big problem.

I shake dirt off my head and give her face a lick.

"Yuck." She wipes her face, and I go back to my task.

She grabs me again and doesn't let go. She carries me over to the hose and sprays me with water. Why? I couldn't tell you. She carries me to her house and holds me with one arm while she gets out a big towel and then dries me off. But she gives me a treat, so I forgive her for interrupting my hunt.

I follow her to the communal kitchen, where Shannon now sits at the computer. She mutters while she scrolls through words on the screen. Nicholas is baking cookies. Oh boy. I lie down in my bed and rest my head on my paws. I listen while I wait.

Shannon looks up from the computer. "Where's Cole?"

I think she's asking me, but I don't know how to answer in a way she can understand.

Elena pulls a piece of paper from her pocket. "Says here he's gone to the hospital to see Donald."

"Why would he do that?" Shannon swivels her chair to face Elena.

I want to tell her, but I can't. I bark, but she doesn't get it. They both look at me but turn back to each other. Oh well, I try.

Elena shrugs. "He doesn't say. Maybe to talk to the doctors. He's been out at the estate all morning." She takes a deep breath. "I didn't mean to get him involved in all this. It's awful."

Shannon gets up and puts her arms around Elena. "And we're no closer to finding Javier, but we will." She kisses Elena on the cheek and lets her go. "Cole is strong. And I'm glad to see him in action again. He needs this. Don't worry about him; he can take it. I'm just sorry to see the price you're paying for his recovery."

Elena smiles and peers at the computer screen. "What's all this?"

"Trying to get a little more background on these Bloomfields. What an odd bunch."

"Tea time," Nicholas sings from the other side of the room.

I jump up to my place, and everyone sits. We nibble treats, and the three of them drink tea. It smells bad and I don't even want to try it. They talk about the history of the Bloomfield family, the wealth they accumulated in the past, some scandals that cast shadows over the family a long time ago.

"Maybe that's why Donald is so secretive. Skeletons in the closet." Nicholas has a funny look on his face. It's sort of like a smile, but his eyes look angry.

"I have a feeling the reason has more recent origins," Shannon says.

When they finish their tea, everybody goes back to work, so I do too.

I station myself by the front gate and wait for Cole. I keep a close eye on the street, looking for any suspicious activity in both directions. A man walks down the other side of the street toward our place. I bark, just to let him know I'm on the job. He keeps walking and disappears down the block. A couple walks by with a big yellow dog on a leash. They're right outside our gate. I've seen them before, but I don't know them, so I bark and bark, warning them off. You can never be too careful.

The man who walked by before is returning. He's still across the road. I lift my head to catch his scent. He's too far away to see him clearly. I growl. I know that smell.

Chapter Eleven

Cole had grabbed his bike and ridden hard, heading straight for the hospital. It was only a couple of miles. Locking his bike up at the stand, he made his way on foot to the ICU. None of Donald's family had arrived but they'd hired two private nurses to tend to him in a glass-walled room off the nursing hub at the end of the corridor. When Cole asked about his condition, they identified themselves, but would not answer his questions. With a little dissembling, like implying that Donald's wife had sent him - well she had, in a way - one of the nurses changed her mind.

She escorted Cole out of earshot of the other nurses at the hub. No, the doctors didn't know what was wrong. They'd run every standard test in the book. They'd looked for poisons, taken x-rays, MRIs, ultra-sound, but still had no answers. They could not stop the internal bleeding, and both Donald's liver and kidney functions were severely compromised. His blood sugar was normal, and the family had insisted there was no excessive use of alcohol or drugs, prescription or otherwise.

"I know this is difficult news for the family, but we are completely stumped," the nurse admitted. "We're consulting with other specialists, and we just have to run more tests. We'll keep looking for the cause and a treatment."

As they went back toward Donald's room, the nurse placed a hand on Cole's arm. "He's been asking for someone over and over again. But we don't know who he means." She looked at Cole expectantly.

"I'll see if I can find out." Cole concluded this was the reason she had spoken to him at all.

She nodded, and Cole went into Donald's room. She returned to the nurses' station at the center of the hub and busied herself with computers and charts.

Donald didn't look much different from that moment Cole had found him on the beach, except there was no blood on him. Instead the blood hung in a plastic bag from an I.V. stand at the head of his bed. A plastic tube snaked from the bag to the needle in the crook of Donald's arm. He was still pale, apart from the purple bruise on his forehead. His breathing was assisted by a pump pushing oxygen into his lungs every few seconds. A plastic mask covered his mouth. It was clear he could not breathe on his own.

A machine at the side of his bed measured his oxygen level, pulse, and blood pressure. Bright red numbers fluttered up and down, never settling into a steady, healthy rhythm. He was in trouble.

"Javier?" His eyes fluttered, barely opening.

It was difficult to understand him with the mask over his mouth. Cole walked to the foot of the bed. "No. It's Cole Steele."

Donald closed his eyes and frowned. He pried the mask from his face. "I want to see the boy."

Cole could barely hear him. "I'm sorry. I don't know where he is."

Donald's eyes opened, then closed again. "Damn." He struggled to breathe and the machine beside his bed began to beep rapidly.

"I was hoping you could tell me where he is." Cole stepped to his bedside and replaced the oxygen mask over his mouth and nose. "But I see it's a mistake to ask you to talk."

Donald scrabbled at the mask, removing it again. "We had coffee. Yesterday, was it?" He held the mask to his mouth and breathed deeply.

"I found you yesterday morning at the beach pavilion."

"You did?" Donald raised his eyebrows, then closed his eyes, and breathed heavily, taking in as much oxygen through the mask as he could manage.

Cole waited. Minutes ticked by with the red numbers flickering up and down on the monitor. Donald seemed to drop off to sleep. Cole had just decided to leave when Donald pulled the mask aside again.

"We had coffee to sign the papers." The mask fell back into place.

"What papers?" Cole could no longer decide what might be relevant. He just kept asking questions. Something that seemed wildly irrelevant might lead him to Javier.

"The botanic garden, of course. You didn't find them?" Donald's lungs labored.

"No. There were no papers." Cole moved closer and replaced his mask. What botanic garden? It was so hard for Donald to talk, Cole didn't ask.

"What about the money?" He talked into the mask.

Cole wasn't sure he heard him correctly Donald's voice was so muffled. "I didn't find any money, either."

Donald closed his eyes and breathed rapidly. Cole waited.

Donald removed the mask once again. "He said the coffee tasted terrible. Spat it out. I thought it was good. My own special blend I'd been trying for a couple of days." He replaced the mask himself this time and closed his eyes.

Donald must be rambling, and Cole could not bring himself to ask any more questions. Cole patted his shoulder. "I'll come back later."

Donald pulled the mask off and grabbed Cole's hand. "He got up to check the beans." Donald replaced the mask. He was definitely rambling now and clearly needed to rest.

Cole turned and started for the door. Had Donald told the doctors or nurses about the beans and Javier's comment? Was it relevant? Cole would pass it along just in case.

"Someone pushed me. From behind. That's the last thing I remember."

Cole walked back to Donald's bedside and put his hand on Donald's shoulder.

"Find him. I need to see him." Donald's eyes closed, and he seemed to sink into the bed.

Cole put the mask over Donald's mouth again and left.

Marco Diary Entry 12

I'm keeping my eye on that guy across the street while I wait for Cole to come home. The stranger is loitering. I know that word. People behind the restaurants used to yell it at me – stop loitering, you mangy mutt. They were always angry when they said that. I'm angry at that man across the street. He shouldn't be there.

I growl but no one notices, so I bark, and keep barking until he looks at me. I wish he was closer; I want to get a better look. And a better smell. Too many scents interfere. Car exhaust, wet cement, cigarette smoke, other dogs – and their pee and poop. I guess some of our neighbors don't pick up after their dogs the way Cole and Elena do for me.

But I still know that man's scent, even though it mingles with all the others. I smelled him at that place where we found that man. Somewhere on those grounds. Everywhere really. On the trails, in the gardens, on the farm, even in that big house.

I wish I had some help. Being chief of security is a lonely job. These are the times when I miss my family. I am really the only one here who takes it seriously, but I can figure this out. Maybe he'll come closer if I stop barking. I tuck myself behind a bush and watch.

The man moves uphill, away from our house. That won't help me figure out who he is. He keeps hidden behind big trees across the road. He's getting further away.

Cole rides up the street. Standing on the pedals as he pumps his way up hill.

The man turns away and trots uphill and out of sight.

I bark and bark, trying to let Cole know we should chase that man. But Cole doesn't understand what I'm talking about. He opens the gate. I try to slip through. He grabs me and hugs me to his chest.

"It's okay, Marco, I'm here. We're safe."

Oh Cole, how I wish I could believe you.

Chapter Twelve

Cole went straight to work the minute he got home. Marco stopped barking and trotted beside him to the kitchen. Nicholas was in the middle of cooking dinner, and Shannon sat at the computer. Elena would be done in the garden soon.

Shannon was making a sacrifice to take so much time away from her office to help Elena. She was always slammed at work. Defense attorneys who cared about social justice always were, especially since public defenders were overwhelmed, and she did a lot of pro bono work.

Marco lay down on his pillow, his chin propped on his paws, watching every move Nicholas made. It must be close to dinner time. Cole was touched that the pup had waited for him by the gate, instead of coming in here as he usually did while Nicholas cooked. Every day he and Marco seemed to bond a bit more.

Shannon swiveled around in the red leather computer chair, as Cole opened a beer and sat on one of the benches at the table. Nicholas set a bowl of roasted hazel nuts, dusted with some Hatch red chili powder in front of Cole. Marco wagged his tail, and Nicholas handed him a tidbit from the chopping board.

"So, what's the story with Donald?" Shannon picked a nut from the bowl.

"He's awake and struggling to breathe. Struggling to remember what happened." Cole cracked nuts between his teeth. "Says he met with Javier that morning to sign papers, and that he brought some money with him. Also says he was pushed, and that's why he fell." Cole took a swallow of beer. "But, one. . ." he held up a finger. ". . . I didn't find any papers or money. And two . . ." two fingers up. ". . . the doc says he wasn't pushed but collapsed and hit his forehead on the table."

Shannon and Cole sat in silence for a minute, while Nicholas sizzled something on the stove. Smelled like onions, garlic, maybe a little rosemary.

"So what papers?"

"Don't know. His only explanation was – 'about the botanic garden, of course'." Cole rotated his bottle of beer on the surface of the table and stared down its neck.

"What botanic garden? There are lots of them. And that's if you only count those around here. In Forest Park. The Japanese Garden. The Chinese Garden. The Rose Garden. Plenty of others too." She waved her hand.

"I know. I have no idea what he was talking about."

"Moving on." She took a dainty sip from her beer stein. "I've been searching out more info on these lawsuits and came across some interesting items. Got a lot of hits on Lexis Nexis about your boy, Donald." She took out her iPad and showed Cole some of the documents she'd downloaded.

Allegations of enormous unpaid debt, fraud, and even corruption appeared in multiple locations. Donald apparently owed millions to several big investment and venture capital firms. And they were going after him.

Cole digested the numbers. "I'm surprised he's not completely insolvent."

"Ah. That's where the fraud and corruption suspicions come in." Shannon slid her finger across the screen to bring up another doc. "He's keeping his lawyer plenty busy."

Cole finished reading, a lot of legalese that left him none the wiser. But he got the gist. "The only potential white-collar crime I don't see is bribery."

"I wouldn't put it past him." She flipped past more docs. "But I am seeing a pattern here. Looks like he's pulling out a lot of cash, which has disappeared. I wonder if he was planning on going somewhere."

Cole lifted a shoulder. "I don't get it. And in all this you found nothing about any botanic garden?"

"Nope." She swiveled back to the computer screen. "I talked to my buddy, Sandi, at the FBI, white collar division. Asked a few delicate questions. Of course, she couldn't tell me anything. But she did tell me why she couldn't say anything – part of an on-going investigation." Shannon leaned back in her chair.

"The implication is clear. Either he or some close associate is under investigation by the FBI." Cole squeezed his eyes shut to think.

"I'd say so."

"What the hell does any of this have to do with Javier's disappearance?" Cole opened his eyes. Seemed like his brain was malfunctioning.

Shannon started clacking at the computer keyboard. "Well, let's look up this unknown but incipient botanic garden." Her fingers flew over the keyboard. "Nothing. And that's odd. They'd need a lot of permits, zoning changes, and such if they were really planning such a thing."

Cole got up, rolled Shannon's chair away from the desk, and leaned over the keyboard. "Blind me with all your fancy legal jargon, why don't you? I've got an easier way. I'm searching the internet for the whole damn bunch."

Cole typed. Not as fast as Shannon, but he was no slouch either. While he searched, Marco darted from his pillow to snatch morsels Nicholas dropped on the floor. Occasionally Nicholas selected a delectable bit and fed it to the pup. After commanding him to sit, of course. Life was pretty good for everyone. Except Elena. Cole's concern for Javier continued to mushroom.

Donald's Wikipedia page was short on real information. Mostly filled with blather, accolades, and sycophantic admiration. Had he written it himself? It never mentioned his date of birth. He genuinely guarded his privacy. Even so, somehow his age showed up from public records – he was sixty-seven.

Cole's search for Blake fetched a lot of information on his company, Blanchard Cyber-security, but very little on the man himself. Despite the bland name, the business had been a leader in the region for a number of years. A small company with only four employees, besides Blake himself. Brenda had also worked there and moved up to vice-president very quickly. Odd that such a small company even needed a vice-president. Maybe Blake had created the position for her. Cole acknowledged the cynical thought. They'd been on the verge of expanding into the big leagues, with a presence along the entire West Coast, when they went out of business.

"The perils of letting one customer eat up your time and resources, I guess." Shannon had been reading over Cole's shoulder.

Besides further information on Blake's business background and the dead reporter's article on the demise of

Blake's business, Cole learned nothing more about the man himself.

When Cole searched Brenda Blanchard (nee Bloomfield), he learned nothing about her cyber-security skills or business acumen. But he did learn that she and Blake had eloped after working for Blake for two years. It was three years ago, when she was just twenty-one. No splashy high-society wedding. Cole guessed Donald disapproved in spite of Irene's high opinion of Blake.

Cole found that Portia, like Donald, had her own Wikipedia entry. Another vice-president in the family, but this time it was of Bloomfield Enterprises. And Portia seemed to have earned it. She sat on the corporate board, of course. She ran meetings and conferences. She met with state officials on a host of policy issues. Like her father, she'd gone to the top business school in the country, where a building on campus was named Bloomfield Hall. Cole discovered one interesting tidbit – Portia was Donald's step-daughter from his first marriage. A marriage that ended when his first wife died twenty-two years ago. Cole found nothing on the deceased wife, not even her name. Odd.

Portia's active social life, covered in minute detail, appeared in many publications, from her ski trips in Switzerland to her cruises on their private yacht along the Riviera. Not as secretive as her dad, obviously. More of a publicity hound. But three years ago, her glamorous jet-set social life had ended. Cole could find no account of why.

He found nothing at all on Krista, and began to feel sorry for the shy, hesitant, silent woman he'd met just the day before. What had happened to her?

There was also little on Charley Hawkins or Reggie Ordway. Hawkins had been a leading horticulturalist, trained at Oregon State University in Corvallis, ran a successful company for years. Went out of business about the same time as Blake. Ordway had kept his head down. All Cole found was an old online yellow page listing for Ordway Watch, his defunct security firm that had died about the same time as the others.

Unwittingly, Cole had saved the best for last. He searched for Irene Bloomfield and hit the jackpot. He whistled.

Shannon pushed him aside. "You look like a giant question mark, hunched over like that. Sit down."

They jostled each other until Cole knew he was beat. "Listen to this." Shannon's voice filled with glee. "The SPCP, Society to Prevent Child Pornography, announced today the receipt of a donation for $100,000 from Mrs. Irene Bloomfield, formerly known as Cindy Slamm, producer and star of adult films."

Marco Diary Entry 13

Seems like dinner is going to be late. Shannon is laughing, but it's not a happy laugh. Cole keeps talking really fast, like he's excited. Nicholas stops cooking and walks over to the computer. They all crowd around in front of the screen.

"You gotta be kidding me." Nicholas's voice booms.

"Okay. What've we got?" Cole is calm now as he stares at the computer screen.

I wait patiently on my pillow and listen.

"She ruled the L.A. adult film world for many years, but abruptly retired when she married the wealthy scion of the Bloomfield family of Oregon." Shannon reads out loud.

"No wonder she's so wary of gold diggers." Cole grabs roasted hazelnuts from the table. I wish he would give me some. Treats would go down well right now.

"Hey. How do you know she was the gold digger? Porn's a billion-dollar industry you know. She could be loaded." Shannon leans over the computer screen. "It goes on to give background on the society. Seems Mrs. Bloomfield was a major donor to this child pornography prevention program for years. Making up for her shameful past?" Shannon steps away and sips her beer.

It would be better if she sits because then I could crawl into her lap and remind her what time it is. But she doesn't. She keeps reading. "In her heyday she produced a series of blockbuster films in the category with her partner, Jackie Stone."

Cole holds up his hand and Shannon stops reading.

"I met a woman named Jackie at Irene's today." Cole says. "They seem to be living together."

All three stand and stare at the computer. I lie down on my pillow again and take a deep breath. Sometimes I have to be really patient.

"Hey, this article is by that reporter who died in the car crash." Nicholas stands with his hands on his hips, like he does when he thinks about his menu. I trot over and nudge him in the back of his calf. He needs to get back to his real work - cooking.

"What's the date on that piece?" Cole steps up and scrolls through the screen. I'm watching closely to see if anyone will ever realize how late it's getting. "Hmm. It's from a year ago." I hear him clicking that plastic thing they call a mouse. It's not really a mouse, and it is no fun to chase, I can tell you that. I bit it once. Big mistake.

"Here's another piece by the same guy." Cole reads silently for a while. I hope he's getting hungry, then everyone might get back to what they should be doing. But no.

"Wow." Cole whistles. "This guy does not hold back at all. Quite a long expose of Irene's career in the porn business. And he put it together with a timeline of Donald's financial misdeeds over the past three years. The business closures, Donald's unpaid debts to that point, the suggestion of impending bankruptcies, potential fraud. Then the capper – this article. Everything seemed to implode about three years ago." Cole clicks some more, and the printer starts up. Dinner is going to be even later.

I hear the door open and I jump up to greet Elena. Finally, we can eat! But she stops in the doorway. The others don't realize she's there, and they just keep talking.

Shannon steps up and takes over at the computer. "I'll get back on Lexis Nexis at my office tomorrow. See what else I can track down. Might find more on the civil side as well as the criminal. In the meantime, . . ." She turns and looks at Cole. "I hate to say it. . . "

Cole nods and sits down on the red leather chair. "I know. We've got to search Javier's background too. See what we can find."

I stand on my back legs and paw at Elena's thigh. She needs some kisses. But she doesn't even notice me. She stares at Cole and doesn't say a word. Uh-oh.

Chapter Thirteen

Elena paled. Cole felt terrible and didn't know what to do. But Shannon did. She walked around him, grabbed Elena by the shoulders, and pulled her close. Neither of them spoke for a long moment.

Marco wrapped his front legs around Elena's calf. He jumped and squirmed and wagged his tail. Nicholas and Cole walked over and joined the group hug. They stood silently, breathing. Marco transferred his grip to Shannon's leg, then Nicholas's, then Cole's. Cole leaned over, picked him up, and put him in the center of the huddle.

Elena chuckled. She backed away, smiling and wiping away her tears. "*Mierda*," she muttered.

They all dropped their arms, and Cole put Marco down. Elena went to the beer chiller, grabbed a bottle, and popped it open. "I can tell you anything you want to know." She sat and sipped.

Shannon grabbed a note pad and pen and sat beside her. "Okay. Shoot."

"Really?" Elena stared down at the table, then looked at Shannon. "Okay. What do you want to know?"

Shannon reached over and patted Elena's shoulder. "We need to know him as well as you do, but we'll settle for anything you want to share. It's important."

"Where should I start?" Elena gave a half-hearted smile.

"When did Javier go to work for Bloomfield?" This whole mess revolved around Donald. So, Cole started there.

"Maybe a year, year and a half ago." Elena tipped her head back and squinted her eyes, then nodded. "Yeah. He started and then brought Tony on a few weeks later."

"Around the time you came here?" Cole asked.

"Don't like this coincidental timing. Not at all." Nicholas's voice boomed, as it so frequently did.

Shannon raised her eyebrows and held her finger to her lips, shushing him. "Use your inside voice."

"Well, I'm just a man." Nicholas's falsetto screech filled the room. It broke the tension, and everybody laughed. Grinning, he returned to his cooking. Marco wagged his tail and followed him.

"Wasn't really a coincidence. I was really pissed at him for taking Tony with him. Not me." Elena's voice was soft.

"Here's what I find suspiciously coincidental - the business failures, the reporter's exposé, and then his death in the car crash," Cole said.

Shannon tapped Cole on the forearm. "One thing at a time." She turned back to Elena. "So how did that come about?" Shannon held the pen poised above the paper. "Javier's getting hired I mean."

"I'm not sure. We had a lot of clients around the area. He'd been doing garden maintenance since high school. I always assumed one of our clients recommended him to Mr. Bloomfield. The first month or so Javier worked there, I had pneumonia and wasn't working. I don't know the details"

"He didn't go to college to study horticulture like you did?" Cole had been impressed with Elena's skill set and knowledge when he hired her.

"He knows as much as I do, maybe more, but he's too impatient. Wanted to earn money, not go into debt. Besides. . ." She clamped her mouth shut.

"What?" Shannon's voice was gentle.

Elena shook her head. "He couldn't get student loans. Wasn't eligible." For the first time since Cole had known her, she sounded bitter.

"Why not?" Shannon maintained a soft, gentle approach.

"He doesn't have any papers."

"What do you mean by papers?" Cole frowned. Was he asking the inane questions again?

"He's not legal." Elena stared at the floor, her hands hanging down between her knees. Marco trotted over and licked her fingers.

"But you are." Her news took Cole by surprise.

Elena nodded. "Because I was born in this country. My brothers weren't. My parents came here illegally twenty-eight years ago. Javier was three, and Tony five." Her voice got quiet. "I was born a year later. In Modesto."

Cole felt like a callous jerk. Why had he never asked her anything about her family? Nicholas, Shannon and he had known each other since college, and Elena had fit right in, so Cole never even thought about her history before they had come together in the compound. At the very least, though, he should have asked these questions when she solicited his help. He'd wasted valuable time. He still didn't know if any of this was relevant, but it could be.

"We moved to Medford when I was ten. And my dad worked in the orchards. Got a good permanent job." Now that she'd started, it seemed she didn't want to stop. "My parents died nine years ago. Javier put me through school. Tony took off." She shrugged and looked up at Shannon. "I loved all the trees, and watching the bees buzzing from flower to flower, and the birds nesting." She smiled. "I guess that's why I chose to study horticulture."

She'd gone to community college and moved to Portland with her brand-new AA degree seven years ago. At twenty she and Javier had started their garden maintenance business. At least Cole had read her resume, even if he hadn't shown much curiosity about her roots.

Cole had hired her a year and a half ago. Damn, there was that recurring time frame. "When Javier went to work for Donald, you came to work for me." It had been the first time in his life he'd had any real money and he had just bought his place here.

Elena finished her beer, setting the bottle down carefully on the table. "Does any of this help?"

"I don't know." Shannon made a few more notes. "It might. Is it possible that Javier got picked up by immigration?"

"Wouldn't he have called me? Or had someone else call? I'm his emergency contact number." Elena's eyes were wide.

"Not necessarily. In fact, not very likely. These days, they take your phone. Hold you incommunicado until they ship you out. No due process. It's barbaric." Shannon's face turned red. "I'll get on it at the office first thing in the morning." Shannon flipped to a new sheet of paper. "I'd sure like to know how he came to be hired at Bloomfield's and why."

Marco Diary Entry 14

I smell anger. It smells like that awful liquid they use sometimes in restaurants to clean. I used to smell it in alleys when I foraged for food. I crawl into Shannon's lap and lift her hand off the paper with my nose. She drops the pen on the floor. She takes my head in her hands and kisses me on the forehead.

"You little scamp." She laughs.

Nicholas is finally cooking again. I think I might starve if he doesn't hurry.

"I'll go back out to the estate tomorrow and track down his employment history. Someone has got to know who hired him and why." Cole pats me on the head and sits down beside Elena.

I smell the food Nicholas is cooking. The nasty smell is gone. I squirm my way out of Shannon's arms, and run over to my pillow to watch Nicholas dish it up. Elena gets up to set the table.

Cole grabs her hand. "I'm sorry our questions are so intrusive."

She stops and smiles at Cole. "How else can you help me?" Her shoulders slump.

Nicholas cooks one of my favorites - meat, the kind they call steak. But I am distracted by Elena's unhappiness. When she finishes setting the table and sits down, I run over and crawl into her lap. I am sure my kisses will help.

Cole moves again to sit next to her. "Is there anything else you can tell me about Javier's relationship to Bloomfield? Anything I can use to leverage information out of them?"

Elena stares at the table, holding me in her arms and patting my sides. "I don't know anything. We didn't talk about it much, I was so angry about him offering a job to Tony instead of me. And Mr. Bloomfield was so secretive. About everything."

She sits very still, then bends her neck to kiss me on the top of my head. "Oh." She looks up at Cole. Her eyebrows are way above her eyes, like she's surprised. "Javier had a locker out there. I don't know what he kept in it."

Chapter Fourteen

Cole hadn't driven this much in years and was weary of the drive to Bloomfield's place even before he got in the car. Marco and he had gone for their morning run just before dawn. The dog pulled Cole directly across the street and spent a lot of time sniffing the base of the trees. He concentrated on one in particular, the one directly across from his compound. Finally, he'd consented to the run, so they'd gotten a late start.

While he drove, Cole berated himself for his incompetence. He should have taken the whole mess more seriously days ago, especially now that he knew how vulnerable Javier really was. To immigration officials, to retaliation from the Bloomfields for some real or imagined revelation of secrets.

Javier could have simply gone underground, but Cole's gut told him Javier was in danger. Cole admitted it, he also blamed Elena. If she'd told him Javier's immigration status and other details from the beginning, he'd have taken the disappearance more seriously.

While Cole muttered, Marco tapped a paw on his arm. When Cole glanced at him, he wagged his tail, then stood on his hind legs with his front paws on the dash board. He stared ahead, scanning for trouble, Cole guessed. Or just curious about where they were headed. Cole told him to sit down.

"That's dangerous, Marco."

Marco ignored him.

Once again Cole drove to the service entrance, since it was easier to enter the grounds there. But this morning the gate was closed and chained. He backed around and made his way to the formal gate at the front where he was buzzed in without identifying himself. Perhaps the camera showed enough detail for whoever manned the security monitors to recognize him. He drove to the ten-bay garage and parked.

Leashed up, Marco hopped out with Cole and trundled slowly to the front door, sniffing every blade of grass, footprint, and step on the way to the portico. Cole found it interesting to observe the dog's process, though Cole had no clue what it all might mean. Cole rang the bell, expecting another long wait. But the door opened quickly. A diminutive woman in a maid's uniform gestured for them to come in. Cole had never seen her before.

"Good morning, Mr. Steele." She led him down the hall to the sunny kitchen alcove. Cole still found it disturbing when complete strangers knew his name. He felt as though he should introduce himself and find out their names. But he kept walking. Portia, Blake, Brenda, and Krista sat around the table over remnants of pastries and coffee. What a nutritious breakfast.

"Sorry to disturb your breakfast." Cole's parents had worked hard work to teach him manners. They'd be proud at that moment. Marco walked away to the end of his leash and sat, keeping his back to them all.

"What can we do for you now, Mr. Steele?" Portia glared.

Probably not much, but Cole didn't say that out loud. "Thanks for your offer to help, Portia." He nodded to her. "Javier Ortega's sister asked me to clean out his employee locker. I'd like to see it, please."

"I wouldn't know anything about that." She turned away and shouted, "Lucinda."

The small woman who'd let Cole in at the front door appeared in the door way. "*Si, señorita.*"

"Please show Mr. Steel out. He's come on a fool's errand." Portia poured herself a cup of coffee. The others looked down at their plates.

"Thank you, Lucinda. I'll be with you in a minute." Cole pulled up a chair and sat on the far side of the table, across from Krista. "Good morning, I don't think we've met." He reached across the table and stuck out his hand. "I'm Cole Steele." He was curious to see if she could speak.

She bowed her head but did not shake his hand. She said nothing.

"Mr. Steele, do not badger my sister." Portia's face reddened.

Badger? By introducing himself? Cole faced Portia. "I'm sorry to hear about your family's financial difficulties."

"They're none of your business." She grimaced.

Cole wondered if anyone else dared speak as long as Portia was in the room. "You're right, they're not. But I still plan to find Javier. And I keep bumping up against your family issues in my search, so I think they may be relevant. Are money troubles the reason you are selling off your furniture?"

"Who told you that?"

"It's a reasonable assumption."

"It would be wrong, however." Portia stood but did not walk away.

"Oh." Cole leaned back with a sudden realization. "It's been repossessed."

Portia slapped the table. "Really, Mr. Steele, shut up and mind your own business."

"I'll be happy to as soon as I find Javier."

"I hope he's dead. I hate that little bastard." Portia radiated rage.

Krista stood and put an arm around her sister's shoulders. She leaned her head against Portia's cheek. Portia remained a ramrod.

An Oscar-worthy performance. Cole decided to keep badgering but aimed his next question at Blake. "What do you know about the botanic garden Donald and Javier planned?"

Portia tore herself away from Krista and leaned across the table. "That was that little bastard's doing. That's what happened to all our money." As she turned away, she slammed into her chair, which tumbled backward, crashing to the floor. She stalked from the room.

Blake and the sisters stared at the floor, refusing to meet Cole's eye. He tried a few more questions, but they stayed mute. Eventually, he gave up and followed Lucinda to the door, with Marco at his heels.

Marco Diary Entry 15

I follow the small woman who opened the door for us earlier. She smells like pork and salsa and tortillas. Nicholas sometimes makes those and calls them tacos. They're very good. My first family made them too. I push ahead to walk by her side and Cole falls in behind us.

She walks quickly, without speaking, leading us to the back door. Not the front. She turns and puts a finger to her lips. "Javier is my friend. I'll show you his locker." She whispers.

She leads us through the gardens, then the tall trees, and the plants with tasty berries. She is going so fast I don't have time to pick any. I'll have to come back later. She leads us to the barn on the edge of the farm.

I don't see or hear or smell anyone today. I find this suspicious. The barn is all closed up and no one is working. The woman stops and stares at the closed door.

"The lockers are inside." She looks at Cole. "I don't have a key. *Lo siento.*" She shakes her head and turns back toward the big house. She waits for us, but Cole and I do not follow her.

"Thank you, Lucinda. We'll take it from here."

"I must get back before she notices." Lucinda walks away.

Cole and I stand still. I lift my head and inhale. None of the workers are here today. That I know. Cole walks around the entire building, while I sniff everything my nose will reach. I smell Tony and Charley, and the workers we did not meet the other day. I get a whiff of Javier. I know it's him because that was the scent all over his house. His odor here is days old. If I could tell Cole I would, but I know he would be disappointed. He wants to find Javier today.

Cole stops in front of a door and reaches into his back pocket. He pulls out a black leather wallet and opens it. He takes out a metal tool and sticks it into a hole in the door. I hear a lot of scratching, then the door opens, and we go inside.

Cole searches with his eyes while I search with my nose. We walk around and around inside the big barn. I pick up Javier's scent again and pull Cole towards one side that is very dark. He trips over something and falls, but I keep pulling. Javier's scent is strong here. Cole scrambles to his feet and we keep moving into the dark recesses beside bags of fertilizers and chemicals. I almost lose the trail. Those odors are so strong. They hurt my nose and make my eyes water. I don't like them at all. Not like the ones Cole and Elena use. They smell good – like chicken and cow poop.

I lead him into a separate room where we reach a long wall made of metal. It has tall metal doors in it. I find one that smells exactly like Javier. I stop and sit down and wag my tail. I hope Cole knows what that means.

Cole takes his phone out of his pocket and makes it into a light. I don't know how he does that. "Ah. The lockers." He whispers.

He takes those tools out again and fiddles with a metal ring on the door. He opens it with a clang and reaches inside. I stick my head inside the bottom and smell something terrible. It reeks of that awful stench at the beach where we found that man.

Chapter Fifteen

Cole found a small canvas grocery bag in the locker and emptied the rest of the locker's contents into the bag. A change of clothes, a jar of seeds, some books, an extra pair of work boots. About what you'd expect. He shined his light around the interior to make sure he'd found everything. The locker was empty. He closed the door, reset the padlock, and began a search of the crowded storeroom they'd passed through.

He discovered bags of synthetic fertilizers and agricultural chemicals stacked to the ceiling. He made a mental note to never eat the fruit grown here and to keep Marco away from those strawberries. Cole took out his phone and snapped some photos. He probably didn't need them but found himself increasingly uneasy. He looked down at Marco. The dog was too.

Cole also found extra parts for farm equipment piled haphazardly against the wall. He guessed Charley and Tony were not giving this job their best shot. He couldn't blame them for that. He found no clue as to why no one worked today.

He crossed the packing area to Charley's office door along the north side of the barn's interior. There was no sign on the door with office hours or why the farm was closed. Just as he took out his lock-picks, Marco pulled the leash taut with a lunge and began to bark. Wildly. Cole tried to quiet him. After all, Cole had broken in and didn't really want to be found. But Marco wouldn't stop.

The door to the outside where they'd entered slammed shut. The lock snapped into place. Whoever had locked them in had surely heard Marco and knew they were inside. Cole called out, but there was no reply. Should he bust out or wait until whoever had done it disappeared? Since Marco and he shouldn't be there, Cole decided to wait.

Cole listened and watched Marco. Cole expected Marco to be on high alert, but he calmed down right away. Cole heard nothing more from outside. He waited a few more beats, then used his flashlight app to examine the door from the inside. He turned the handle below the lock and pushed. The door opened about an inch then stopped.

"You have got to be kidding me." Cole swore. Marco barked. One sharp indignant demand. He pushed his nose into the crack between door and door jamb, while Cole searched along the inch-wide opening. He saw a hasp and padlock.

Cole pondered the situation, then used his light to return to the chemical and equipment room. He left the bag of Javier's belongings with Marco next to the partially open door. The dog kept his nose wedged in the open crack and growled.

Cole found a rusty hacksaw in a box of tools in the storeroom. It wasn't the right tool for the job, but he couldn't find a bolt cutter. Better than nothing. He brought it back, managed to slide it through the gap, and started sawing his way through the padlock's shackle. This could take the rest of the day, but he kept at it, since he was out of bright ideas.

Marco lifted his head and growled again. He stood and faced the store room, his body rigid. He barked. He sniffed, nearly hyperventilating.

Cole caught a whiff of what he smelled. Smoke.

He took out his phone and dialed 9-1-1. Told them he needed a fire truck right away. The volunteer fire station was right down the road. Not far. He'd seen it when they drove out to the island, and it was a must in farm communities. Even so, Cole looked for a crow bar or large piece of lumber, anything he could use as a lever. He found both – a 2x4 and a rusty crow bar. He wedged the 2x4 under the door and pushed, trying to leverage the door open. It barely budged. He slipped the crowbar between door and jamb above the hasp. He smashed down as hard as he could in the confined space. Metal on metal reverberated into his hands and up his arms. Marco barked. He didn't stop.

Smoke began to swirl from the storeroom into the open packing area where they stood. Cole slammed the crowbar into the hasp again, felt it give a little. Marco stopped barking and pushed his nose into the slightly wider crack. His little body strained, and his feet scrabbled on the ground. Cole smashed the hasp again. It gave a little more.

Sirens screamed. Cole slammed his shoulder into the door. Again, and again. Each time the door moved slightly, the gap widening. Marco pushed along the bottom of the door, his body rigid, his feet digging into the floor. What a valiant little dog.

Sirens died away as the rumble of fire truck engines neared. Doors slammed. Booted feet hit the ground. Marco wagged his tail, gave an exuberant yip. Cole stepped away from the door and ran at it full tilt, smashing into it with his shoulder. The hasp broke free, the door swung open and

Cole fell to the ground. Marco ran to him and licked his face. Cole laughed.

"Mr. Steele?" Ordway stood over Cole.

"Yes." Cole looked up.

"How'd that happen?"

"No idea. Don't you know?" Cole scrambled to his feet. Marco started growling, very low in this throat, a thrum in his chest.

Ordway stood still, silent.

Cole turned to watch the fire fighters at work. Ordway seemed spectacularly disinterested. Anger bloomed in Cole's chest. What the hell kind of security guard was this guy, anyway?

"Ms. Bloomfield sent me to find you." The guard started down the path back toward the gardens.

Cole followed for a few feet. The head of security for the estate was walking away while a building burned? It made no sense. "Hey, Ordway." He shouted.

The guard turned around. "Yeah?" He squinted. "I'm supposed to take you to Ms. Bloomfield's."

"So I gather." Cole nodded. "Did you see anyone around?"

"Nope." The man turned again and kept walking.

Cole looked back at the barn. The fire was nearly out. Since the firefighters had everything under control, Cole grabbed the bag and followed. He figured if their investigators wanted to talk to him, they would call. He sure as hell wanted to talk to them as soon as he got the chance.

Who the hell had locked him and Marco in and started that fire? And which Bloomfield had sent the guard? Cole had never heard Ordway refer to Portia or her sisters as Miz, and Irene was a Bloomfield in name only. When they reached the fork in the path, where one way led upstream to

Irene's and the other branched to the left, straight to the main residence, Cole got his answer. Ordway stopped and pointed the way to Irene's, then turned and walked toward the big house.

Cole paused and looked at Ordway's retreating back. "Thanks." His sarcasm left the guard unmoved.

He waved over his shoulder and walked on.

Marco pulled Cole eagerly toward Irene's. Cole held the leash in his left hand, trying to ease the throbbing pain in his right shoulder. He guessed the pup actually liked her, but Cole couldn't see why. Maybe it was the treats. Cole found her grotesque, allowing her husband to paint those portraits of her children and who knew what else. Before the two reached the front door, it opened, and Irene ushered them in.

"Well, I guess that walking turd is good for something. He finally fetched you. I told him to bring you here as soon as you arrived." Irene led the way to the sitting room.

They sat as they had before, Cole in the overstuffed wing-back chair, Irene on the sofa with Marco beside her. She gave him a small dog treat, which he took delicately from her fingers. A tea set with two cups already sat on the coffee table.

"What did you want to see me about?" Cole wondered if she knew about the fire, and, if so, why it didn't concern her at all.

"Since we're skipping the pleasantries, Mr. Steele, I'll get straight to the point." She frowned. "I understand you've been looking into our finances and private affairs."

"Have I?" Cole settled into the chair, wincing when his shoulder came in contact with the chair's back.

"Now that you know all about us, I want to know more about you, and why you are snooping." She straightened the collar of her blouse. "Who do you think you are?"

"A friend of Elena Ortega, Javier's sister." Cole leaned forward, relieving the pain in his shoulder slightly. "Did you know Javier and Donald planned a botanic garden? Did you know they met on the morning I found Donald on the beach? Did you know your husband was going broke? And that Portia blames Javier?" Cole's questions spewed faster than she could answer. He paused.

She glared at Cole for a long time. She looked just like the step-daughter she seemed to hate. "Nothing goes on around here without my knowledge." She hissed just as Portia did.

"And approval?" Cole surmised what she had left unstated.

"Just so." She nodded and leaned back.

"Tell me about the botanic garden."

She laughed. "Oh, that was all make believe. He had to launder his money somehow. That poor boy didn't have a clue."

"You think this is funny?" Cole tried but failed to keep the outrage out of his tone.

She scooted forward on the couch and poured them each a cup of tea. "You take yours with cream, if I remember correctly." She handed Cole a cup. "It certainly is not funny, Mr. Steele, and I apologize for my misplaced levity."

Cole put the cup down. If he hadn't, he might have thrown it at her head. "If you know all, who locked Marco and me in the barn, and started the fire?"

She looked puzzled. "Are you hurt?"

Cole ignored her question. "And since you approve all, how can you stand to look at those portraits of your daughters?" He reminded himself she was once an actress. Maybe that gave her too much credit. How much acting was required of a porn star?

"What?" She set her own cup down and stood. "What portraits?"

"The ones in the upstairs family room. One of each of you. Scantily clad, like models on the runway. One, in particular, is really weird. Krista sitting in Donald's lap. An adult but dressed as a child beauty queen."

She actually looked shocked. Her face turned red. Her jaw tightened. Cole thought she might have a stroke. He hated to admit it, but he was pleased by her reaction.

"I'll kill that son of a bitch." She started toward the front door but stopped when Jackie walked in from the hall.

"Too late." Jackie took her hand. "Sit down." She led Irene back to the couch. "He just died."

"Damn." Irene smiled.

"Can't get no satisfaction." Jackie sat down beside Irene and grinned.

Marco Diary Entry 16

I jump up beside Irene, this kind woman who gives me treats. I lick her hand just once to remind her that I'm waiting for another. She settles into the pillows behind her back while her friend, Jackie, sits on her other side. Cole frowns at me. I want to reassure him, but he doesn't understand much of what I tell him. I'm patient. He'll learn.

When most people learn that someone they know dies, they are sad. Irene isn't sad.

She looks away and takes a deep breath. "I don't believe what you're telling me, Mr. Steele. No such portraits exist." Irene's voice sounds harsh.

Maybe Cole is right. I jump down and go to him. Cole always tells the truth. She shouldn't talk to him that way. I don't like people who are mean to Cole.

Cole reaches into his jacket pocket and pulls out his phone. "See for yourself." He pokes the phone with his finger and hands it to Irene. "Go ahead, scoll through."

I am not sure I trust Irene anymore. I lean against Cole's leg to listen while Irene and Jackie stare at the phone screen.

"He always told them they had to be tens. Forcing them into plastic surgery, starvation diets. Damn that man." Irene draws in her breath sharply, again and again. She turns red. She might faint. I stand on my hind legs and tap Cole on the thigh. To warn him. She is in trouble.

"Irene?" He leans forward.

Irene doesn't answer. Her eyes close and her head falls back against the couch. Jackie's eyes are wide. She presses two fingers on Irene's wrist and looks at her watch. Her lips move but I don't hear her speak. Cole is silent as well. After awhile, Jackie takes a deep breath. "It's okay . . . she's okay."

Cole leans back again. "I'm sorry."

Jackie puts Irene's hand down on her lap and pats it gently. Irene doesn't move. Her eyes stay shut and she breathes slowly and deeply.

"It's not your fault, Mr. Steele. Irene has to watch her blood pressure and heart rate. Sometimes she forgets to monitor her emotions." Jackie squints. People sometimes do that when they're worried. "She has atrial fibrilation. It gets triggered by extreme emotion."

"I had no idea I would trigger such emotions. Should we take her to a doc? The E.R?" Cole stands and moves toward the two women.

"She'll be fine in a minute. But I'll get her pills to be safe. Will you stay with her?" When Jackie stands I jump up beside Irene and lick her fingers. She smiles and carresses my head. She's not sad, but she's still angry. That's not good for her heart, so I lay my head in her lap and remain very still. It will help calm her down.

"Of course." Cole sits down again and stares at Irene while Jackie walks down the hallway. I breathe slowly and deeply, showing Irene what to do. She keeps her hand on my back, feeling my reassurance. It's helping.

There's a sharp knock on the door. Cole gets up to answer it, but Irene and I don't move. A fireman wearing a bulky yellow coat, rubber boots, and helmet comes into the sitting room. He takes his helmet off and looks around the room, first looking at me and Irene and then turning to

Cole. I lift my head and sniff. He smells like smoke and sweat and acrid chemicals.

"You Cole Steele?"

I lay my head back in Irene's lap. She needs me more than I need to check out this stranger. Cole can handle him.

"Yeah." Cole nods, then glances at Irene. "Maybe we should take this outside. Give me a minute. I want to make sure Ms. Bloomfield's okay."

The fireman steps further into the room. "What's the problem?" He pulls a microphone that's attached to his shoulder toward his mouth. "Got an E.M.T on the crew. Should I call him?"

"Please." Cole nods.

"Not necessary." Irene opens her eyes and looks at them. She sits up. "Come." Her voice commands attention. And obedience.

Cole and the man come closer. "Sit," she says. I sit up, but neither man does. "Suit yourself. Tell me what happened."

"I've got some questions for Mr. Steele here." The fireman puts his helmet on the coffee table and takes out a small spiral note pad. "Give me your account of the incident." He looks at Cole.

Cole tells the man a short version – that we had gone to the barn to empty Javier's locker as his sister had asked us to. When we tried to leave the exterior door was locked, and then we smelled smoke.

"I busted the door down just as you guys arrived. That's it. Good thing you were close. And not out on another call."

"Did you go into the store room where the equipment and chemicals are kept?"

"Only to look for a tool to get the padlock open."

I don't know why Cole is not telling the whole truth. He must have a reason, but he always tells the truth. I don't like this.

"Not earlier? Before you found the lockers? We came across an awful lot of dog foot prints in by the stored supplies." The man's eyebrow's are drawn together, like he's angry or suspicious.

Cole shakes his head. I bark to remind him we always tell the truth. He looks at me, smiling, and puts a finger to his lips. "Hush."

"We know you studied to be a chemist." The fireman shrugs. "Among other things. It'd be mighty easy for you to start a chemical reaction with the items stored in that barn."

"Why would I do that? And how did I lock the two of us in there, with a padlock on the outside?" Cole raises one arm and holds out a hand with his palm up. He sounds like he is about to laugh.

"Well, someone did. And you and your dog are the only ones who went in there today." The man is still writing notes as he talks.

"What is your name, sir?" Irene's voice is loud in my ear, since I am in her lap.

Jackie walks in with a glass of water before the fireman can answer. "Quiet down, Irene. Here's your medicine." She frowns when she sits down beside Irene. Jackie hands Irene a pill and the glass of water. I sniff the pill before she puts it in her mouth.

"Now, sir." Irene puts the glass down on the table beside her. "Name and badge number, if you please."

"Sergeant Collins. 94531." He has an angry stare. "Want me to spell that?"

"Jackie, please write that down." Irene stares just as hard at the fireman. "Thank you, sir. Now, don't be absurd. Mr.

Steele would have no reason to set our barn alight, especially if he risked his own life and the life of this sweet little innocent." She pats me on the head again. I don't like people to touch my head, but now is not the time to interrupt.

"I don't concern myself with motive at this point. I'm simply looking at the physical evidence."

"Keep looking, then. You're missing something." Irene sighs and leans against the back of the couch.

"Such as? Anything you know about the incident?" The sergeant's pen pauses over his paper.

"We can't do your job for you, Sergeant, but how about a timer? Or a detonator outside the building?" Jackie snorts. She's annoyed.

"Can we talk outside, Mr. Steele?" The fireman puts his paper and pen in his pocket.

"I think that's wise." Cole takes the fireman by the elbow with one hand and picks up the man's helmet with the other. He looks at me. "I'll be right back. Stay with Irene and Jackie please." He leaves with the fireman.

I don't like it. My job is to keep my family, even if new family, safe. But I do as he says. I lay my head down in Irene's lap again and keep my eye on the door. This is bad.

"Irene," Jackie takes Irene's hand. "I'll go take a look at those portraits. I don't want you to see them."

Irene nods. "Yeah. I'd like to know how the hell that happened. And why the hell Blake didn't tell me about them."

Chapter Sixteen

Marco, tail wagging, met Cole at Irene's front door. The dog clawed at Cole's leg, Cole's shoulder complained when he picked up the pup and walked to the arm chair. He settled with Marco on his lap.

"I'm pretty sure you can expect a visit from the fire marshall later." Irene looked at Cole with a sour expression. "What a jackass."

"Just doing his job." Cole shrugged off any suggestion of incompetence or colusion. "They'd have to do a lot of convoluted thinking and evidence tampering to prove I locked myself in."

"That's their specialty." Jackie snorted. "Especially if Portia wants them to come after you."

"I find that far-fetched." Cole grimaced, leaning back to ease some of Marco's weight off his arm.

"She provides the entire funding for the station and their salaries." Irene frowned. "Actually, Bloomfield Farms does, and Portia lets them know they would get nothing if not for her."

Despite Irene's remarks, the accusation still sounded absurd. "You didn't know anything about those paintings?" Cole picked up his cup of tepid tea. He drank, worrying about whether he should raise the topic again.

Irene sipped her tea. She made a face. "In fact, Donald mentioned wanting to do them and I expressly forbid it."

"And you expected him to obey you?" Cole found this both fascinating and weird.

"Of course." Irene shifted her weight and looked away. So she was either lying or fooling herself. Cole didn't know which.

"Mr. Steele." Jackie spoke sharply. "Let's drop this discussion for now, shall we? Irene needs to rest." She stood and took Irene's arm, helping her stand, then guiding her toward the hallway. "I'll take Mr. Steel to see Blake and the girls. I'll get you some answers." Her voice was hard as diamonds.

Irene walked down the hall without looking back.

Jackie turned to Cole. "Shall we?"

Marco jumped up as Cole stood. The three of them went back to the main house along a narrow trail toward the front of the property. It was a trail Cole had not stumbled upon before. Western red cedar and larch towered overhead, casting shade in which rhododendron and sword fern thrived. This oddly peaceful haven at the center of the troubled family and their estate made him uneasy. Dissonant and ominous. His skin crawled.

Jackie marched in the front door like she owned the place. They found the three sisters sitting once again in the triangle of gilt chairs in the barren living room. It was as if they held regular prayer meetings of a secret cult in this room. Creepy.

Portia looked up, anger firing her eyes. Brenda smiled at Jackie. Krista looked away, her mousy brown hair falling across and hiding her face.

"What are you doing here?" Portia's shock was all too evident. Cole couldn't tell if she was surprised to see him or Jackie.

"Where's Blake?" Jackie barked at Portia, ignoring her question.

Portia stood and walked toward Jackie and Cole, her face flushed. "He's making funeral arrangements for my father."

"Your stepfather." Jackie's harsh tone showed no mercy.

"How dare you?" Portia quavered.

The two women glared at each other and said nothing more. What a bizarre exchange. Who were Portia's real parents? Did it matter? Though he had yet to find Javier, Cole regretted his involvement with this discordant family. He waited, letting Jackie take the lead.

"I won't ask you again." Jackie turned away and marched toward the hallway and the grand staircase to the second floor. Marco leapt ahead of Cole to follow Jackie. The pup pulled Cole in his wake. Cole didn't hesitate. Jackie took the stairs two at a time. Marco galloped behind her, and Cole brought up the rear. No need to hurry.

Cole had just reached the landing at the top, with Marco's leash tight as a bowstring, when Jackie grabbed the first painting she encountered and wrestled it off the wall. She lifted it over her head and slammed it over the newel post. Cole hadn't noticed before that she had the biceps of a wrestler. The canvas tore, and the stretcher bars shattered. She let go and went on to the next painting.

Cole stepped back into the sitting area and gathered Marco to his side. He watched the one-woman demolition derby, her face distorted in rage. When she finished, she stood back with a triumphant glare.

Cole admitted to sharing her sense of satisfaction but found the extremes of her behavior and emotional turmoil alarming. That not one member of the household had appeared to stop her frenzy struck him as beyond odd. Maybe they'd called the cops and retreated to a safe room.

That would have been the sane thing to do, but no one in this family was sane.

An eerie silence fell. A door latch down the hall clicked, hinges squeaked until a narrow sliver opened in a doorway. An eye appeared in the crack. It stared at Jackie. The silence broke with a burst of laughter from the room behind the partially opened door. Jackie's laugh joined in. She doubled over as her laughter overwhelmed her. The door opened, and Blake stumbled out, still laughing.

"Ding, Dong, the warlock's dead." Blake sang. He marched down the hall humming the tune from the Wizard of Oz. "Thank god," He added, as Jackie's laughter subsided.

They looked at each other, then turned and looked at Cole.

Cole made no comment. He just wanted to help Elena and get the hell out.

Blake's face grew serious. He walked over and took the other easy chair. Jackie sat on the red leather sofa.

"Maybe Javier did us all a favor." Blake looked at Jackie when he spoke.

Jackie shook her head. "There's no evidence that Donald was killed."

"There's no evidence of anything." Blake sniffed. "Which is my point. No reason at all for his death. Massive internal bleeding. Cause unknown." He used air quotes.

"But no poison in his system." Jackie grimaced.

"Nothing traceable anyway." Blake smiled. "Don't get me wrong." He turned to face Cole. "If I knew where Javier was, I'd thank the guy. But I haven't got a clue."

"Do you record video from your surveillance cameras?" Cole steered away from this alarming conversation.

Blake shook his head. "We only have the one at the main gate, anyway. And that's only to see who buzzed the intercom."

Soft footfalls mounted the carpeted stairs, and Brenda appeared. Her eyebrows rose as she took in the splintered stretcher bars and shredded canvas. "Oh, thank god." She joined Jackie on the sofa.

"If you hated them, why did you sit for yours?" Cole blurted.

Brenda waved her hand in a gesture reminiscent of her mother. "Oh, I didn't. None of us did. He made up this shit in his own teeny, weeny little brain."

"That wasn't his only teeny, weeny organ." Jackie chuckled.

Cole settled back in his chair, careful to protect his injured shoulder. He tried to disappear. Let them talk and see where it led. Marco jumped into his lap, circled a few times, and settled with his head propped on Cole's knee. Marco stared at the three of them.

Jackie glanced at Marco and made kissing noises toward him, then turned away. "So, how's the wicked witch of the east taking all this?" She took Brenda's hand.

Since they both smiled, Cole assumed she referred to Portia.

"Devastated, of course." Brenda's gleeful expression said it all.

"What about Krista?" Jackie actually looked concerned.

Brenda screwed up her mouth and shook her head. "About what you'd expect. Uncertain. Afraid. Looking for a way out of Portia's control."

"Victim psychology 101. Now that the primary bully is gone, his henchman, or in this case, woman, steps in." Jackie's face clouded. "Bitch."

"I think she may have found her way out." Blake spoke softly, as though afraid to be overheard. Had Cole's tactic succeeded? Had the man forgotten Cole sat right across from him?

"What do you mean?" Brenda frowned.

"I found this love letter in Krista's room." Blake reached into his breast pocket, removed a plain piece of paper, and unfolded it.

"Let me see." Brenda leaned over and grabbed it from Blake's hand. She scanned it quickly.

"What's it say?" Jackie peered at the paper.

"'You are my own true love. Be brave.'" Brenda laid the paper on the coffee table.

"Who wrote it?" Jackie snatched it up.

Brenda shrugged.

Cole bet Irene knew, but he didn't make a sound. He wanted to hear more.

"She always got the worst of it from your dad." Jackie dropped the note back on the table. "The nose job when she was only ten. The boob job at sixteen. Body shaming her whole life."

Blake looked away. "The son-of-a-bitch thought if his daughters were beautiful, like skinny fashion models, it raised his standing. Made him a better man."

"Sicko." Jackie squeezed Brenda's hand. "But you know all this too well. No need to dwell on it now. You're free. Free at last." She glanced at Cole, and he got the message.

Brenda let go of Jackie's hand and stood. "I don't know what to tell you, Mr. Steele. Javier's not here. Hasn't been for days. I think you need to look elsewhere. And if Blake's hunch is right, I think you shouldn't look too hard."

Cole stayed in his seat. "Why did Donald fire Javier?"

Marco lifted his head and stared at Brenda.

"Did he?" Brenda looked at Blake, who shrugged. "If he did, it was Portia's doing. She hated Javier. Thought he was stealing from us."

"Was he?" Cole wanted to keep them talking. No one answered. "Okay. Why did Donald hire him in the first place?"

Blake stood and took his wife's hand. "Can't help you. We've got a funeral to arrange. Krista to rescue from Portia's grip. Show yourself out." The two of them disappeared down the stairs.

Jackie sighed. "I can help you there. Donald didn't hire Javier. Irene did."

Marco Diary Entry 17

Irene's friend, Jackie, leads the way back to the cottage in the woods. I take my time, even though I know that Cole is in a hurry. I have investigating to do. I don't like being ignored. He's not learning what I can do fast enough. I pick my way along the trail. I gather all the scent tracks I can find and memorize them. I smell Jackie, Irene, and Blake on this trail. They walk here every day, going back and forth.

On other days in these woods Cole and I walked two other footpaths. Those have traces of other scents. I need to go back to those trails. I can pick up scents for weeks, but only if it doesn't rain too much. So far, we have had only sunny skies. How can I get Cole to understand I need to do a thorough investigation of those trails to find out who walks them and when?

At Irene's cottage Jackie leaves Cole and me in the living room again and goes to check on Irene. She should take me with her, so I can check on Irene too, but she doesn't. I wait patiently with Cole. I sigh. There are no cookies. Cole doesn't drink any of the tea that still sits on the coffee table. If they only drink tea, why do they call it a coffee table?

Irene and Jackie come in and sit on the sofa together. Irene is pale. I look up at Cole so that he will unhook my leash. He gets the point, and I trot over to Irene to see how she feels. I sit in front of her and put a paw on her knee. She invites me up, and I wiggle my way between her and Jackie. I lay my head on her knee. Yes, she's feeling better.

"Jackie has filled me in on what happened at the big house. I apologize, Mr. Steele." Irene draws in a long breath. "I should have told you about Javier from the beginning. I hired him to rehabilitate my cottage garden. He brought his brother, Tony, along, because his sister was ill."

I wonder why this is a secret. I expect Cole to ask, but he stays silent.

"He's a fine young man. We had lunch together daily." Irene smiles at Cole, but his face doesn't change. "He told me his background. How happy he was to be in this country. How proud he is of his sister. He's very ambitious, as I suspect you know. He'll go places, I'm sure." Irene stops speaking and closes her eyes.

Her heart speeds up, so I know she's not telling the whole story. I lick her hand and push my nose under her fingers. She pets my head and her heart slows. That's good. I don't want anything bad to happen to her. Cole and I need more information. And I like her. I think about how I can get her to tell Cole everything.

Jackie shifts in her seat. Maybe she will tell us more. "We thought Javier should go to work for Donald too. The estate grounds needed help. Charley's a good farm manager, but careless about the private gardens."

"So, Donald hired him, just like that?" Cole looks at Jackie.

"No. Not just like that. But he was always easy to manipulate, if you knew how to appeal to his ego. Irene and Blake make a good team." Jackie stands. "I'll get some fresh tea, shall I?"

I hope Cole says yes, because we'll probably get cookies, too. And I could use a drink. But Jackie doesn't wait for Cole to answer. She leaves the room, and the three of us sit in silence. It's a nice silence, and Irene's heart rate is slow and steady.

"We do make a good team, Mr. Steele." Irene opens her eyes again. "When that rat bastard put my darling daughter out of business, after I had successfully gotten her out of his clutches, I knew I had to do something."

"Such as?" Cole tilts his head to one side.

"I'd set Blake and Brenda up in the first place to get her out of here. They were doing just fine. But that shithead went after them." Irene is not answering Cole's question. She's repeating something she already told us. I sit up and stare at her, and her eyes soften. She sighs. "I may have made a few suggestions to that jackass that he'd raise his status if he funded a botanical garden here on the estate." She wagged her head back and forth. "And I may have suggested that hiring a nice Mexican boy to run it would make him look magnanimous. Blake helped me sell the idea. He handled all the paperwork."

"Portia had a shit-fit, of course." Jackie carries the tea tray into the room and sets it down. There are two plates of cookies and a dish of water. I wag my tail. Jackie is smart. "She doesn't like anyone getting close to her precious papa. Just ask Irene."

Irene laughs. The kind of laugh that is angry, not happy. "She certainly succeeded in driving me out of the house." Irene looks at Cole for a long time. "If you really like snooping so much, you might want to look into what happened to Donald's first wife, Portia's birth mother."

"Why?" Cole leans forward to prop his elbows on his thighs.

"Portia's mother and Donald married when Portia was thirteen. Her mother disappeared six months later." Jackie frowns as she pours the tea.

Chapter Seventeen

What did these tangled, unhealthy relationships and family history have to do with Javier? Cole needed tangible information, not conjecture and paranoid fantasies dredged up from the past. "Tell me more about Javier and the botanic garden. I can't see Donald spending money on such a venture."

Irene smiled. "So, our sordid history doesn't interest you?"

Cole shook his head. "Not in my wheelhouse. What do you take me for? A gossip columnist? A Fox news analyst? All I want is to find Javier."

Irene handed Marco a cookie from one plate and took one for herself from the other. She didn't offer Cole one.

"Tell him about it." Jackie offered Cole the cookie plate – the one for humans. He didn't take one.

"Oh, all right." Irene sounded like a petulant child. "Donald's creditors have been hot on his heels for some time. And he'd stupidly shafted some of his biggest investors." She glared at Jackie, who nodded. "I convinced him to siphon off cash from the business and give Javier the money for the garden to hide it from the creditors."

"A simple solution." Jackie smiled.

It didn't sound simple to Cole. "And that's why Portia thought Javier was stealing from the family coffers." He didn't need to ask. He knew the answer.

Irene bobbed her head. "Blake may have given Portia that impression. To keep the focus off the real plan. After all, the garden was a ruse. None of us wanted a garden. We just wanted Donald's money."

Cole looked around, wondering if any of them had any conscience at all. Using anyone in their clutches to get hold of Donald's money. And now that he had died, how would the estate fare? And how would they all survive without his wealth? Seemed risky, betting on this house of cards. A convoluted way to finagle money from a man who was supposed to be the sharpest, most successful businessman of the times.

Cole had no interest in the family intrigue unless it led him to Javier. But every time Cole asked where the man was, he got no answers. Donald was dead. Was Javier? The question niggled its way into Cole's thoughts. "Give me something I can take to Javier's sister. Something useful, for God's sake."

Irene raised her eyebrows. "I don't understand why you keep harping on Javier's whereabouts. Especially since his sister surely knows he'll be back tomorrow."

Cole leaned forward. "What?"

"He's on a business trip. He'll be back tomorrow. I'm sure he told his sister all about it. He tells her everything."

A new question raged in Cole's head. Why had no one, including Irene, mentioned this earlier? He did not believe for one second that Elena knew and had sent him on a wild goose chase. Cole asked a different question. "Where did he go?"

"I'll not tell you that. But I will say that he's running an errand for me and is scheduled to return tomorrow afternoon. He should be back by three o'clock." Irene clamped her lips together and leaned back.

Cole shook his head, frustration at a boiling point. "When did he leave?"

"Five days ago." The corners of Irene's mouth turned up in a perfect illustration of smug.

"You sent him away the day Donald fired him?"

Irene nodded.

"But he met Donald for coffee day before yesterday. The day I found Donald at the beach pavilion."

"What?" Irene looked at Jackie.

"You think he double-crossed us?" Jackie spoke barely above a whisper. "Or came back and left again?"

"Certainly not." Irene grimaced. She turned to Cole. "You are mistaken, Mr. Steele."

"Maybe." Cole shrugged his one good shoulder. "But when I visited him in the hospital, Donald told me all about his meeting with Javier on the morning I found him."

Irene kept shaking her head.

"He also told me someone knocked him down."

"Who?" Jackie's voice was sharp.

"He didn't know."

"Another one of his 'poor me' stories, no doubt." Irene flapped her hand toward Cole. "Probably lying about Javier being there at all. Pay no attention to his lies."

"If Javier went away, why was his phone in the garden?" Cole's voice rose along with his impatience with Irene's dissembling.

"There's a simple explanation. Most likely he dropped it on his way out of town. I did ask him not to take it with him."

"Why would you ask him to leave his phone?" Cole took a deep breath. And why would he leave it in the garden and not at this house? Cole didn't ask that out loud.

"So he couldn't be traced, of course. That should be obvious, even to you, Mr. Steele." Irene's eyed him with a smirk on her face. "I do hope I haven't caused you or Elena any unnecessary concern."

Her false sympathy threatened to make Cole do something he would regret. He clamped his mouth shut, feeling boxed in by walls of lies. Marco barked. Just once. Cole didn't, though he felt like it. Despite the gray hair and plump grandmotherly look, Cole was up against a world-class liar. He needed usable data points to chart a new course. He pondered in silence. Some time passed. He wasn't even sure how much. Without another word, Cole stood, grabbed the canvas bag, and walked out. Marco followed. Cole had the leash in his hand but didn't hook it to the pup's halter.

Cole marched down the path toward the barn, Marco at his heels. If Jackie told the truth about the fire department, and Portia had the kind of influence Jackie claimed, then the fire marshal might not investigate the fire properly. Even though Cole doubted her story, he decided to have a look around. Perhaps he wasn't in the best frame of mind to look for clues, but he didn't give a damn at this moment. He'd had it. And he had to get something for Elena.

All evidence of the fire department's presence was gone. They'd not even taped off the scene. One wall of the barn – the back wall against which the chemicals had been stored – was blackened by soot. It was still damp. Marco hesitated to follow Cole through the opening where Cole had knocked the door down earlier. Marco stood on the threshold, one paw raised, neck outstretched, and sniffed. His nose twitched. He snuffled.

Cole dropped the canvas bag next to the pup and kept walking, picking his way over debris scattered by the firefighters as they'd worked to douse the flames. He had no idea if he'd discover anything useful, but he had to see what he could find. Jackie's claims, even if false, had shaken Cole's confidence in the fire investigators. But if what Jackie said was true, they'd only uncover whatever Portia wanted them to. If Jackie was full of shit, it would do no harm to have a look.

No smoke lingered, but a sour odor filled the room. Probably why Marco remained at the door with his nose in the air, refusing to follow. Cole picked his way to the storeroom. The air quality deteriorated. He probably should have worn a mask, and he was glad Marco stayed where he was. Charred bits of plastic bag lay scattered across the dirt floor. The remains of the fertilizer and compost bales that came wrapped in plastic.

Shelves to the side contained lumps of melted plastic – the gallon jugs that once held pesticides, rodenticides, and fungicides. Had all those liquids volatilized or were they now saturating the ground beneath his feet? Cole shuddered. What had he imagined he would find? He took out his phone, turned on the flashlight app, and peered along its narrow beam. One area appeared more damaged than the rest, surrounded by burned wooden shelving and hardened globs of plastic. Cole assumed that's where the fire started.

He closed the flashlight app and opened the gallery to compare what he'd seen earlier with what he saw now. The bags of chemicals had been rearranged. He crouched and examined each piece of plastic, each fragment of charred wood, taking pictures the whole time with his phone's camera. He finally spotted something useful. A cigarette butt. Burned nearly to its filter. Sitting on one of the charred shelves.

Cole had seen the "no smoking" signs that first day he met Charley and Tony. He'd seen Charley's reaction when Tony lit up a cigarette outside the barn, and later had played with his lighter in Charley's office. Cole doubted this butt got here because someone stepped in here for a smoke. It could be a fuse of sorts. An oldie but a goody. It worked. There'd be no way to identify the brand or who had left it there, but it could have been used to start the fire. Cole had confirmed to his satisfaction that the fire had been deliberately set. No accident. And no coincidence that Marco and he were locked in when the fire started.

Marco Diary Entry 18

I wait for Cole by the door. He shouldn't be in there. It's dangerous. I should go to him, protect him, and lead him away. But the air hurts. It burns my nose and eyes, and, now, my lungs. I bark. I try to tell him to come back. I wait. He isn't coming, so I bark some more, my voice rising. I act like demons are on the way, that we are in danger. Because we are.

Good. He's coming. He runs toward me and scoops me into his arms. I lick and lick his face. I saved him. I am so happy. He picks up the bag of Javier's things and carries me away a few yards, then puts me down. He starts to attach my leash, but I dance out of reach. I trot down the path toward the beach. I stop and look back at Cole. He stands still, staring at me, but his eyes are blank like he's not seeing me. I bark to get his attention.

"C'mon, Marco. Let's go this way." He points up the path toward the car.

I bark again and sit down. He shakes his head. I wag my tail.

"This way," he commands me.

I give up and follow him back to the car. I have to think of a better way to tell him we need to go back to the beach. I jump into the front seat, then stand with my front feet on the dashboard. I want to know where we're going. Maybe home. It's past lunchtime.

But he turns in a different direction. I sniff the air. We've been this way before. He drives, and I look for dangers out the front window. I can always warn him with a bark or growl. It's a good system. I didn't invent it, but I've used it for a long time.

He turns up a dirt road. Yes, we've been here before. I smell Javier's scent as we turn into the drive at his house. I wag my tail and crawl over Cole as he opens the door. I jump out and run circles around the house with my nose to the ground. Javier has not been here since we were. I am disappointed. I want to find Javier because Cole wants to. And because Elena is sad. She's afraid for her brother.

I slow down and sniff the ground more carefully. Someone else has been here. Recently. I stop where the scent is strongest. I huff up the air. Dust and leaf litter sticks to my nose. I smell Tony, who we met at the barn. Tony smells a lot like Elena and Javier. That makes sense because he is their litter mate. I follow Tony's footsteps. I go slowly and carefully, so I don't lose the scent. I look up to see Cole watching me. Good, he's finally learning to appreciate my work.

I follow Tony's trail to the back of Javier's house. It stops near the place Elena and I crawled under the other time we were here. I stop and look at Cole. He stands without moving. Watching. I run to him, jump up on my hind legs, and scrabble at his knees. Then I crawl under the house. I bark when I reach the compartment that Elena and I found. Cole crawls under with me. The door to the compartment is open and I stick my head in. I huff up more scents. I smell something strange. It's not a snake or rat – I know those smells by heart. It's not even another animal. But it is something I've smelled before. People's hands often smell like it. It's the green and white paper they carry in their pockets to exchange for food and other things. I've heard them call it money.

I pull my head out and growl, so Cole knows there's something important he needs to look at. He pushes me gently aside and shines a light inside. He takes a long time looking at every corner and crack in the cubicle. Finally, he breathes out sharply. He reaches in and pulls out a tiny piece of paper that was stuck in a crack. He shines the light on it. It's a piece of money. Cole's eyebrows scrunch up like he's puzzled. He puts the scrap of paper in his wallet.

Chapter Eighteen

The gang at home had just finished lunch when Marco and Cole arrived. Nicholas looked up, his mouth full of pie made from the fresh strawberries Elena had picked that morning. He grinned, catching errant strawberries that fell into his hand, and stuffing them back into his mouth. Shannon slapped him lightly on his arm. Elena laughed. Cole was happy to see everyone in a lighter mood, and that Elena's gloom had lifted slightly. What a lucky man he was to have such friends.

Marco raced to the table and jumped up to his place. He found only an empty bowl, and looked sharply at Shannon who sat to his left. He whined and wagged his tail. When she didn't produce his food immediately he pawed her arm until she dropped her fork, loaded with pie, onto her plate. Marco laid his head on her forearm and snuffled, rapidly inhaling the aroma of strawberries and ice cream. He whined again.

Shannon laughed. She patted his side. "Hold on, you little squirt. I'm not your servant, you know." She walked to the warming oven and removed one plate. She picked up another from the butcher block counter next to the oven. She set the warm one at the head of the table for Cole, and the other in front of Marco. He waited, looking at Cole expectantly.

"Okay." Cole nodded.

Marco dove in and cleaned his plate – a tablespoon of salmon, an ounce of sliced green beans, and a quarter cup of dog crunchies – before Cole even had a chance to rummage through the freezer looking for an ice pack.

Cole left Javier's canvas bag on the sideboard next to the espresso machine. He wrapped the ice around his shoulder and sat. Needless to say, the salmon *en papillote*, dressed with hollandaise, the sautéed *haricot verts* and red new potatoes were exquisite. And not just because he was ravenous after his morning's adventures.

Shannon wrinkled her nose. "Dear God, Cole, you stink." She leaned to her right and sniffed Marco. "You do too, Marco." He licked her nose.

Cole told them about their morning at the Bloomfield estate. The fire, Donald's death, the demolition of the portraits. It seemed a lot for half a day. He left out some of the details he wanted to skip in front of Elena - Javier's potential role, the corner of the $100 bill he'd found under Javier's house. He was afraid of causing her even more pain. He'd talk to Shannon about that later. In private. Cole could not say out loud that Blake and the others accused Javier of killing Donald and stealing the money for the botanic garden.

Cole waited to shower until after he'd had his piece of pie a la mode. Elena kindly took Marco to give him a bath. Cole rushed back to the kitchen after he'd bathed and strapped up his shoulder. He wanted to talk to Shannon. He figured he could beat Elena back because Marco hated bathing and it took a while to calm him, wash him thoroughly, and dry him off. Cole returned to find Shannon and Nicholas deep in conversation. They looked worried.

"What's up?" Cole grabbed an IPA from the chill chest and another ice pack from the freezer. He balanced the ice on top of his collar bone to ease the pain. The beer wouldn't do any harm either. He sat beside Shannon.

"The fire marshal called while you were in the bath." Shannon picked up a note she had scribbled. "He wants a call back. An interview, he said, not an interrogation."

Cole took the note but put it down without reading it. "It's a load of crap. Marco and I were locked in. I busted us out."

"They don't seem to believe that." Shannon cocked her head to one side. "So that's what's wrong with your shoulder." She balled a fist and punched him softly on the other arm. "Is Marco okay?"

"He's fine. I am too. Thanks for asking." Cole repositioned the ice pack and winced.

"Yeah, right. I can see that for myself." She smiled. "So why do they think you had something to do with the fire?"

Cole shrugged. "They knew I'd studied chemistry. Thought I'd have the knowledge to put together the right cocktail of chemicals to make fire, I guess." Cole stopped. "Come to think of it, how did they know I'd studied chemistry? How'd they know anything about me?"

"You're kinda well-known, at least locally. That big article about you and your invention for the military. The miracle fabric you created. I mean a thin-as-silk flotation device, body armor, and wet suit that prevents hypothermia – that's pretty awesome. Makes good copy." She winked. "Your fifteen minutes."

"Yeah, that's me, the unknown celebrity." Cole changed the subject, launching into a quick report on Blake and Brenda's suspicion that Javier had killed Donald and stolen the cash earmarked for the botanic garden.

"Sounds like typical misdirection to me," Nicholas boomed. His usual response to hearing news he'd rather not hear. "I'd suspect any of those whack-jobs before Javier."

"But we have to take it seriously." Shannon frowned. "Do the police suspect that Donald was murdered?"

Cole shook his head. "Because of the circumstances they did an autopsy. Cause of death was massive internal hemorrhaging. No final results yet, of course, but the docs could not spot a cause for that. They'd already checked for poisons and drugs while he was under treatment. They found nothing."

"Will they do further toxicology tests?" Shannon's eyebrows drew together.

"So far the police don't think it's murder. But the coroner will likely want to dig deeper." Cole took a swig of beer that was getting warm.

"Are the police looking for Javier?" Nicholas had started growling his questions.

"Not that I know of." Cole took the last sip of tepid beer and decided to switch to coffee. He couldn't afford to get sleepy.

"We gotta find him first, brother."

"Absolutely." Cole glanced at the door to make sure Elena had not returned with Marco. "Irene – the Bloomfield matriarch – said a strange thing."

"Only one?" Nicholas sneered.

Cole ignored the joke. "That Javier is not missing. That he's expected home tomorrow."

Nicholas exploded out of his chair. "Where is he?"

"She wouldn't say. Only that he was running an errand for her."

"God damn. And she never mentioned this earlier. To ease Elena's mind." Nicholas looked ready to tear someone's head off.

"But. . ." Cole held up his hand, and Nicholas sat again. "She was surprised when I said Donald had told me he met with Javier the morning I found him at the beach pavilion. She suggested it was one of Donald's lies."

"Oh, this is just so damned convoluted." Shannon sipped her macchiato.

Exactly, Cole thought. "I don't want to say anything in front of Elena but look . . ." he drew the fragment of money from his pocket. "I found this in the hidey-hole under Javier's house."

Shannon frowned as she took the paper from his hand. "Not good. But let's not jump to any conclusions."

Cole retrieved the canvas bag of Javier's belongings and unloaded the items inside onto the table. Shannon grabbed a legal pad and pen from the desk and brought them over. As Cole examined each item, she listed them on her pad. They worked in silence. A Seattle Mariners baseball cap, a sweaty and tattered bandana, a similarly well-used pair of leather work gloves, a pair of steel-toed work boots, a glass jar full of some kind of seeds that looked like small pinto beans, a battered paperback book with a lurid cover, a batch of papers wedged between pages in the middle of the book.

They stared at the assembled items. It made Cole sad. Shannon picked up the papers and unfolded them. Her eyebrows drew together as she read through them. "Legal documents. A contract between Donald Bloomfield and Javier Ortega. They establish a partnership, with Javier as managing partner in Bloomfield Botanic Gardens, LLC. Not a 501-C3, you'll notice. A for-profit theme park of sorts."

She pulled out subsequent sheets. "Attachments." She laid them out one by one for them to see. They were sketches for the gardens. An elaborate labyrinth, a miniature golf course where the hazards and tricky shots would be played around miniaturized waterfalls and northwest plants – dwarf redwoods, cedars, and ferns.

"Not exactly a botanic garden." Cole set the last sheet back on the table.

"Doesn't seem like Bloomfield was trying to hide money from his creditors either. More like he planned to create a different kind of going concern." Nicholas finished looking at the sketches.

"There are too many loose threads for this tapestry to hang together." Shannon tapped her yellow pad. "Irene Bloomfield and her pal, Jackie, enlisted Javier to siphon money away from Donald." She started a new list on a fresh sheet of paper.

"Blake and Brenda were in on this scheme, but Krista and Portia were not. Charley and Tony apparently did not know about the ruse but were stealing small amounts of money by cooking the farm books." Cole added to her list. "And they're starting a cannabis grow operation with Javier, who claims the seed money is coming from Bloomfield himself."

"Are these papers meant to establish a front for the cannabis operation?" Nicholas sounded incredulous. "I mean – why? It's legal in Oregon."

"Good question." Shannon stared at the list. "The security guard, Ordway, doesn't seem to know anything about . . . well, anything. Except he didn't trust Javier." Shannon paused, giving Nicholas an opening.

"Irene hated Donald." Nicholas was growling again.

"So did everyone else, except Portia and, maybe, Krista." Cole threw up his hands. "Does any of this get us closer to finding Javier? That's the only reason any of us are involved." He banged his fist on the table.

Nicholas sat next to Cole and glowered. Nicholas tapped the yellow pad in front of Shannon. "You left one item off your list. The torn corner of the c-note Cole found at Javier's house."

"And . . ." Shannon started writing again. "Javier is missing and so is the money."

Marco and Elena walked through the door. Marco ran to Cole and hopped into his lap. He was clean and dry and snowy white except for the hint of his cinnamon mustache. He squirmed and licked Cole's face. Marco seemed pleased with his new look. And he didn't smell of smoke or chemicals. Elena hung back by the door. Had she heard Shannon's last item?

Cole tried to decide what to do. Couldn't make up his mind, so he took a page from Shannon's book, with a variation of his own. He got up, grabbed a bottle of Elena's favorite beer, Alaskan Amber, and put it on the table. He sat, and Marco settled again in his lap. Cole waved her over. "C'mon. We're brainstorming here, and we need all the gray cells we can muster."

Elena looked at Cole suspiciously, but walked over and joined them. She scanned Shannon's notes, then started to go through Javier's things from the bag. She picked up the torn corner of the bill, looked at it, then shrugged. She shuffled through the sketches for the gardens. "Javier would never go for this. Not possible."

When she picked up the jar of seeds, Marco lunged across the table. He started to snarl. Loud and vicious. He was frantic. Cole had never seen that behavior before. He grabbed Marco and held on. The dog barked and tried to squirm out of Cole's arms. He put Marco on the floor, but he jumped up beside Elena, scrambled over the table again, and knocked the jar from her hand. It landed on the table but didn't break.

Cole folded the pup in his arms again. "It's okay. We're safe." Cole spoke softly, trying to calm Marco. He whined but didn't bark again. No one touched the jar, and that seemed to satisfy him.

"That was weird." Cole looked at Elena. "Do you know what kind of seeds those are?"

"I'll have to look them up." She rose to walk over to the computer. She typed in her search term, and the rest of them waited while she paged through hundreds of images.

Marco lifted his head and looked toward the door. Someone banged on it. Marco growled. Before anyone had time to respond, Tony walked in.

Marco Diary Entry 19

"What the hell are you doing here?" Elena stands by the computer.

I growl at Tony because Elena is angry. He shouldn't be here. He shouldn't make Elena unhappy. They both stand still and stare at each other. Neither speaks. I don't like this.

Cole is still holding me, so I wiggle and push against his arms until he puts me down. I run toward Tony, just to sniff him but he steps back. I smell his fear. I bare my teeth and growl again. Maybe he'll go away and stop bothering Elena.

Cole stands and walks slowly up behind me. Good. Now I have backup.

"It's okay, Marco. That's enough." He bends over to pat my side. "What do you need, Tony?"

Tony looks down. "Sorry. I just need to talk to Elena. It's about Javier."

Cole turns to Elena. "What do you think?' His voice is quiet.

She frowns but doesn't say anything. Everybody stays silent and no one moves. I trot to Elena and paw her knees. She sits down suddenly in the computer chair and I jump into her lap. I lick her fingers. There's a little bit of salmon on them.

"I guess you better leave." Cole grabs Tony by the elbow.

"No." Tony shakes off Cole's grip. "Elena." He calls across the room. "We have to talk."

"Why?" Elena sounds furious. I feel what she feels. She doesn't trust Tony and neither do I.

Tony walks further into the room. Nicholas stands and bars the way. He's much bigger than Tony, and with his wild hair, angry face, and bulging muscles covered in tattoos, he makes his meaning clear. Tony stops moving.

"I'm sorry, *hermana*." Tony peers around Nicholas to see Elena. "We really need to talk."

I feel Tony's fear, so I know he's being brave.

Elena shifts her weight under me, knocking me a little off balance, but I don't fall. I lick the side of her neck, so she knows I'm here for her. Also, so she remembers not to drop me. That tense silence fills the room again.

Elena takes a deep breath. "Okay. Talk." She leans back and tries to cross her arms, but I am in the way.

Tony steps around Nicholas and stands beside the table. Nicholas cups his hand on Tony's shoulder and forces him to sit. Then Nicholas sits close and props his chin on his fist, elbow on the table and glares, but doesn't say anything. He's good at glaring. I'm happy he's protecting Elena.

"You need to know about the deal Javier made." Tony sounds hesitant.

"What deal?" Elena looks at Shannon. "Is that what you three were talking about just now?"

Shannon shrugs. "I'm not sure what Tony is talking about."

"So, tell me about it." Elena puts me down on the floor and crosses her arms. I think I better stand by her, just in case.

"Before I tell you, I want you to know he took me on at the Bloomfield's to protect you."

Elena makes a face. "Yeah. Right." Then she goes quiet and stares at Tony.

"It's true."

"You've never told the truth in your life." Elena's eyes fill with tears. She looks down at me. I put a paw on her knee.

"You know we worked for Mrs. Bloomfield in her gardens."

"Yes. I did know that." Now Elena is angry, not sad.

"Well. That's how this whole mess got started. She persuaded Javier to work for Donald and help her get money from him." Tony keeps talking. "He did it to get the money back for me and Charley. They cooked up a great scam."

Coles sits down on Tony's other side, trapping him against Nicholas. "We know something about that. Irene filled me in this morning. Why didn't you tell me about it when I saw you and Charley at the farm?"

"Who is this guy?" Tony points a thumb at Cole but looks at Elena.

"My boss." Elena smiles at Cole. "And my friend."

"So, how was I supposed to know that?" Tony leans back but doesn't get very far since Nicholas and Cole crowd him. "Charley and me, we didn't know who this nosy a-hole was. Why would we trust him?"

"Maybe because I told you Elena was worried about Javier, wanted me to help find him." Cole is angry. Tony better watch out.

Tony lifts one shoulder. I can tell he's afraid but pretends he isn't. That's not too smart. "Okay. I get it. I screwed up. But here's the thing. Charley and I didn't know about his deal with Mrs. Bloomfield. So, we helped ourselves to the fund we have for farm equipment. 'Cause we want our money back. When Javier told us to quit, he also filled us in on how much money he'd gotten his hands on."

"That's when you decided to start your own cannabis grow?" Cole frowns.

"Yep." Tony squirms. I can tell he's trying to give himself more room. It's the same thing I do when Cole is holding me, and I want to chase deer. "But here's the thing. That dick-head, Ordway, told Donald all about it. That's why I texted Javier. To warn him."

"You wrote – 'shits about to hit the fan'?" Elena is frowning too.

Tony looks back and forth between Cole and Elena. "Right after that he called me again. Said it was a done deal. He was fired."

"That was five days ago, Tony." Elena stands and walks to the table opposite Tony. "Why are you telling me about this now? When you know we've been looking for Javier?" She props herself on her arms and leans across the table. I feel her fury.

Tony leans back. "This is the important part. Javier got all that money in cash. And now it's gone."

Chapter Nineteen

"Son of a bitch." Nicholas stood, grabbed Tony by the collar of his T-shirt and pulled him backwards off the bench. "That's the important part?"

Tony landed on the floor. He stayed down. A wise choice.

"Where the hell is Javier?" Nicholas spit the words between clenched jaws. Cole knew from experience Nicholas was working hard to control himself. Cole laid a hand on his friend's forearm. Neither Shannon nor Elena moved. Nicholas turned Tony loose and stepped back. Tony chose to stay on his back. Submission was the right call. He was smarter than he seemed.

Nicholas stormed to the far side of the kitchen, then turned around and stomped back. They all waited for him to contain his anger. He didn't flare as much as he used to, but he could still be dangerous.

Cole looked down at Tony. "How do you know the money is missing?"

Tony and Nicholas stared at each other. No one moved. Finally, Nicholas nodded.

Tony slid away from him, and then sat up. "'Cause I checked the hiding place. The money's not there." He scuttled backward until his back came up against the wall.

"Under his house?" Cole stepped closer.

Tony nodded.

Elena straightened and moved around the table. She stared down at Tony but didn't speak.

Marco walked stiff-legged toward Tony. The dog sniffed loudly. He stopped a couple of feet in front, half-way between Tony and Cole. He remained rigid, then growled. Elena squatted beside Marco and touched his side. He relaxed. Marginally.

"I don't get it." Tony squinted at Elena. "Javi tells you everything. Why are you pretending you don't know where he went or when he'll be back?"

"Hold on." Cole took another step until he towered over Tony. Cole wanted him to feel threatened. "Irene says Javier's due back tomorrow, but you saw him two days ago."

"No." Tony shook his head. "I called him. Left him a message. Never saw him. And never heard back. I didn't know he'd left town. He never told me anything about leaving town."

"But you had his phone." Cole kept his voice low.

"I told you. I found it." Tony's eyebrows shot up.

"But you are a liar," Elena whispered.

"Me? I know Javi talked to you about everything. Second time he called me he said he was on his way over here to see you, to make some arrangements." Tony started to stand. Not so smart after all. Nicholas, fists clenched, took a step toward him.

"What arrangements?" Elena's voice shook.

"Don't know. Last time I talked with him, he said he was on his way over here." Tony repeated his story, looking back and forth between Elena and Nicholas. "Like I said that was five days ago and I haven't talked to him since."

"That second call – it's not in the call log." Cole spoke through clenched teeth, frustration boiling over.

"Yeah. 'Cause he called from Mrs. Bloomfield's." Tony had begun to whine.

"Could be true. Could be total bullshit." All Cole could think about was how many liars he'd encountered. Hard to keep them straight without a scorecard.

"That's it." Nicholas walked slowly to Tony's side, lifted him up by his shirt front like Tony was a rag doll. "You're outta here." He set Tony on his feet, started to shove him toward the door.

"Wait. Did you see Javier after you sent him that text?" Elena walked over and stood beside Nicholas. "What are you keeping from me?" She turned and gestured toward Cole. "From all of us?"

"*Nada.*" Tony squinted. "And what are you hidin' from your friends?"

"Out." Nicholas dragged Tony over the threshold, tossed him to the ground, and slammed the door.

Elena leaned down and patted Marco. Cole sat down at the table again with his coffee. Nicholas went back to the sink and started washing dishes. Shannon looked down at her yellow pad and stared at her notes. They all breathed again, despite the heavy stillness.

"Okay." Shannon tapped her pad with her pen. "What have we got?"

"Sounds like Donald really did fire Javier." Cole cocked his head to study Shannon's list. "Also sounds like that five-and-a-half-minute phone call may have been to Donald. Have you had any luck tracking that down?"

Shannon shook her head. "If it was Donald, what did they talk about for five and a half minutes? And why did Donald text - 'see me now' – five days later?"'

"And why did Javier say he was coming here, if Irene had actually sent him on an out of town errand and didn't expect him back before tomorrow?" Silence followed Cole's question while he pondered the one, he did not voice but that was at the front of his thoughts – had Javier killed Donald and made a run for it with a bag full of cash?

"What's the latest from the police on Bloomfield's death?" Elena's soft voice floated into the quiet.

"There's no evidence that he was killed." Shannon's eyes flashed, her voice firm. "Javier did not kill him."

"What was the errand?" Nicholas finished drying his hands and tossed the towel over a rack to dry. He walked over to the chill chest and took out a pint of Guinness Stout. Old-fashioned taste, though he drank it chilled.

"And why didn't he tell me about it?" Elena sat again at the computer.

A charged silence returned to the room. They all knew Shannon could be wrong. Despite the lack of evidence, someone may have killed Donald. And despite their protective feelings for Elena, that someone could have been her brother, Javier.

"Okay." Nicholas grabbed a jar of his home-made pickles and a tub of peanuts, walked to the table and sat. "Let's face what's on everyone's mind." He popped open the lid and poured pickles into a bowl. He set the tub of peanuts on the table. "What if Javier stole the money and ran?" He held up a hand. "I'm not saying he killed anyone, but what was to stop him if he found Donald like that? Or if Irene is right and the meeting is a pack of lies? And it was Donald's invention?" He pushed the peanuts toward Elena. "Where would Javier go?"

The three of them stared at Elena. She looked down, then met Cole's eye. "To my *tia's* house."

"Where's that?" Shannon's ability to question gently was one of her best skills.

"Mazatlan."

"Have you called her?" Shannon picked up her cell.

"No. I didn't want her to worry. And she would have called me if Javier showed up. I think." Elena looked at the phone in Shannon's hand for a minute before taking it.

Elena had a long conversation with her aunt while Shannon and Cole filled in the blanks on her list. It struck Cole that they really needed to reconstruct Javier's movements before Irene sent him to Vegas. Where was he when he got Tony's call? Had he returned to the estate? Had he seen Donald? Or Irene? Cole shook his head as if that would clear his thinking. Ha.

"Let's just follow the money for now. They all had great motives to kill Donald. But the police have no evidence he was murdered, and they're not investigating." Shannon tossed her pen on the table.

Elena said her goodbyes to her aunt and returned Shannon's phone.

"Sounds like you had a great talk." Nicholas was as fluent as Elena. "Didn't mean to eavesdrop. Sorry."

"It's okay." Elena smiled. "We needed to catch up. We haven't talked in a while. She hasn't heard from Javier, or me for that matter, in six months. Long time."

"So where does that leave us?" Cole looked at Shannon.

"Damned if I know." Shannon picked up her notes and began to reread them.

Marco barked. He jumped up to his place on the bench, putting his paws on the table. He looked at Cole, then slowly edged his way across the table top to the jar of beans. He pushed the jar with his nose moving it closer to Cole. When it was close enough for Cole to reach, he stopped and barked again.

"Oh, yeah. We haven't identified the beans yet." Cole picked Marco up and set him down on the floor.

"I forgot. Tony messed me up. Again." Elena went back to the computer and resumed the search she'd begun before Tony showed up. Minutes ticked by as she clicked one image after another, shaking her head as she concluded there was no match. She had enough experience to recognize the minute differences in the beans' appearance.

Cole read over the notes Shannon had made. Nicholas munched peanuts and sipped beer. Marco jumped down and stood next to Elena.

She gasped. They all looked up. Marco ran to Cole's side.

"Castor beans." Elena turned to Cole. "Deadly poison."

Marco Diary Entry 20

Finally, Cole understands what I can do for him. I jump into his lap, wagging, happy, and I lick his face. He laughs and hugs me. Now he needs to take me back to that beach, so I can show him everything.

Shannon picks me up and kisses me. I lick her face. When she puts me down again, I dance on my hind legs across the room and paw at Nicholas's knees. He leans down, laughing, and ruffles my ears. I run to Elena. She sits quietly at the computer. She's not smiling. She's not happy. Tears roll down her cheeks. I jump into her lap, but she doesn't hold me.

"Why did Javier have these?" She holds the jar out and looks at Cole.

"Don't jump to any conclusions." Shannon's voice is stern, like it is when she tells me to stop barking.

"He may have planted the seeds on the estate." Cole walks over and puts a hand on Elena's shoulder. "It's a beautiful plant."

Elena puts me down and turns back to the computer. "Look. The symptoms of castor bean poisoning." She stands and gestures to the screen.

Cole steps forward and reads out loud. "Internal hemorrhaging, exsanguination, organ failure." He steps back. "It's untraceable."

Chapter Twenty

Cole frowned. This was not the information he hoped for. He turned toward the others. Elena's skin paled.

"Aw hell." Nicholas marched to Elena and grabbed her by the shoulders. Cole was convinced that Nicholas thought it would comfort her. But she turned away as Shannon stood and enveloped her in strong arms.

"Like I said, let's not jump to conclusions." Shannon's soft voice projected calm. "Sit." She pulled Elena back to the table and gently urged her to sit on a bench. Elena complied, though her body went rigid, her face blank.

Nicholas strode to the liquor cabinet and poured out four snifters of brandy. As if that would help. He set three on the table, then downed his own in one gulp. So much for savoring the flavor and fragrance.

The other three didn't touch their glasses. Cole read the rest of the posted article on castor beans. Wasn't castor oil a medicine? How could it also be poisonous? He scanned the information quickly, his chemistry background making quick work of the technicalities. Several factors determined whether it became medicine or poison. Most relevant, he discovered – it took three days of ingestion before it became deadly. Hadn't Donald said he'd just found a new coffee blend he liked? Could that blend have included castor beans? And if it did, who'd put them in the mix? Was it from ignorance or motivated by malice?

Elena stirred and looked at Cole, her eyes pleading. He wasn't sure what she asked of him, but he had to do whatever that was.

"It's gotta be about the money." Cole sounded hesitant, unsure of himself. That wouldn't help. He cleared his throat. "If Donald was murdered, who gains?"

Shannon straightened. "Yep. Always a good place to start. We'll follow the money."

"Which money?" Elena laid a palm on Shannon's arm.

"We'll start with the estate. Who inherits?" Shannon crossed to the computer and began a search of public records.

With the keyboard clacking and the rest of them silent, Cole grew increasingly uneasy. Could Javier – with his knowledge of plants, his entanglement in Irene's scheme to steal Donald's money, his own plan to open a new business – could he have murdered Donald? Cole didn't know the guy, only his sister, so how could he dismiss the idea entirely? He glanced at Elena. She stared steadily at him. Cole saw the conflict in her face. Familial love and trust battled with the circumstances and doubt. What a terrible position to be in.

"Shannon's right. We're not jumping to any conclusions." Cole sounded confident. That's what he was going for. "Whatcha got?" He leaned over Shannon's shoulder, even though he knew she hated that.

She swiveled around in the chair, knocking him aside.

"Well, that's interesting." Cole whispered. Despite her maneuver with the chair, he'd seen what she'd found the same moment she did.

"Irene owns the estate." Shannon said.

"No one will inherit it?" Elena's voice shook.

"Apparently not." Shannon kept scrolling through the records.

Cole returned to his seat at the table. Marco had found a patch of afternoon sun across the room and dragged his bed into it. He lay with his head perched on the edge, eyes open, watching Cole.

Restless, Cole stood again and walked up behind Shannon to peer over her shoulder. This piece of information negated all Cole's assumptions that Irene, with Blake and Brenda's help, had set up the elaborate scam to steal Donald's money, to get rich off the man's family wealth and business empire. Irene had claimed their goal had been to steal the money she felt was rightfully due to Blake and Brenda, Charley and Tony for Donald's deceitful business practices that had destroyed their businesses. But that seemed like a lie. Or did she need the money to keep the estate going? But she could have sold it at any time, if she really just wanted the money. It was entirely within her power.

It now seemed likely that Irene had decided to ruin Donald for revenge. She'd said so, now that Cole thought about it. The botanic garden scheme hadn't been about the money - she'd said – they just wanted to ruin the son-of-a-bitch. Had she decided that wasn't enough? And they'd killed him? The clicking of the keyboard was like a metronome, both hypnotic and compelling, urging him to keep going, to delve deeper. To mine for some insight that eluded him.

Shannon clicked on screen after screen, but Cole followed the track she traced. She searched Donald's financial records, finding more evidence of lawsuits, and deep debt, creditors that were closing in, federal investigations of fraud that seemed stalled. She found details of his business dealings, his expenditures, and how he spent his time. Mostly on the golf courses in which he owned some share.

How she got into these records Cole didn't know and didn't want to know. He assumed she had the ability to skirt the edge of legitimate and illicit, to delve into gray areas where lawyers and criminals met, the intersection of law and outlaw. He really, really didn't want to know. He just hoped that their own internet firewalls were impenetrable.

Cole watched as Shannon hacked into Donald's personal server. One almost certainly set up by Blake's cyber-security company. Had Blake and Brenda deliberately done a poor job? Shannon found Donald's personal calendar with appointments, meetings, lunches, and social engagements. She clicked on all those that covered the past month. Nothing was entered for the morning Cole had found Donald on the beach.

Shannon moved ahead in time to the following week. In two days' time Donald was scheduled to fly somewhere on a chartered jet. Shannon clicked on the link in the entry. It took her to the company's website. And the flight plan: leaving from the private air strip at PDX, arriving at Carrasco International in Montevideo, Uruguay, with one stop in Mexico City. Two passengers.

Cole reached out and touched the screen. "Who's he taking with him?"

Shannon turned to face Cole. She scowled. "You mean, who had he planned to take?"

"Yeah, maybe. It doesn't matter." Cole wiped a hand across his face.

Shannon read what she'd found aloud. Nicholas picked up a second glass of brandy and handed it to Elena. She put it back down, bent forward, gently placing her forehead on the table. "Who made the reservation?" Her voice was muffled.

Cole took over at the computer while Shannon rose to sip her brandy. Clicking through the records, Cole found the original reservation. "Entered the day he fired Javier." Cole scrolled down the screen. "Called in by Portia Bloomfield."

"So maybe that's who was going along?" Shannon poured herself another brandy.

Elena got up, took a glass from the cupboard and filled it with water. "What do we do now?"

"Time to call the police." Shannon set her full glass down on the table.

"Why?" Elena sipped her water.

"Because we know about the castor beans." Shannon looked at the floor.

"Wait." Cole left the computer and went over to the table. "Javier's supposed to be back tomorrow. Give me a chance to talk to him first. I'll go back out to Irene's this afternoon. If he's really running an errand for her, she'll know how to reach him."

"That's a really bad idea, Cole." Shannon downed her glass of brandy.

"Please." Elena placed her hand on Shannon's arm then turned to Cole. "I'm going with you."

Marco Diary Entry 21

I lie in my bed. The sun feels good, but my people are unhappy and agitated. I know why but I don't know how to help. I stretch and yawn, get up and turn around a few times, then settle again. This helps me think. I watch Elena. Her eyes are sad. I'm thinking about how to make her smile again. It won't be easy.

She stands, and without saying a word, leaves the room. Even though she closes the door, I jump up, and slip through my dog door to follow her. I run to her side as she makes her way to the potting shed. This is a place we like to be together. We can tidy up, put flowers in little pots, look at seeds, and decide which ones to plant. I like keeping up with all the garden chores.

Elena opens the door and holds it open for me to join her. She smiles and bends over to pet my side. "Okay, little sweetheart." She looks around the room. "I think I'll clean myself up."

I know I can help cheer her up.

She sits on a hay bale to unlace her boots. Grunting, she pulls them off and then her socks. I run over and lick her toes. This makes her laugh. See? I know exactly what to do.

She talks to me while she rummages around in her cupboards where she keeps some extra clothes. She finds a clean pair of jeans and running shoes. She tells me how much she misses her family, and Javier. She's worried, she says.

I listen, but I also investigate something that's not quite right. It smells like Javier's house. I sniff along the wall where she and Cole keep fertilizers and bags of soil. No, it's not there. Keeping my nose to the ground I cross to the other side of the shed. The smell is stronger here. I know that scent. It smells like the piece of paper Cole and I found under Javier's house. I snuffle under the potting bench. There's a big roll of cloth there. I push it with my nose. It's heavy.

Elena is still talking to me. Telling me Javier must be okay. He wouldn't leave her. But why hasn't he called? I stop listening. I grab the thick canvas with my teeth. I growl and pull as hard as I can.

Elena laughs. "Oh, you silly one, what have you found?" She puts on her shoes and comes over to me. Kneeling down she ruffles the top of my head. "What is it, Marco?"

She helps me unroll the cloth. She falls back on her butt when it comes loose. She's not laughing now. Her eyes are big. She picks up a handful of paper, a handful of money. The money that smells like Javier. Elena starts to paw through the piles of money bundled with rubber bands. She's breathing fast.

"Oh my God, Marco." She can hardly talk. "What the hell?" She pulls out one bundle with a different piece of paper stuck to it. She stares at it.

"Sorry I missed you." She reads to me. "Don't tell anyone you found this." She pulls me into her lap. "Oh, *mi hermano*, what have you done?"

She puts me down, pulls the cloth up and over the pile of money. She pushes the big bundle further under the potting bench, then stacks empty pots in front of it. She stands, slapping her pants, cleaning the dust off her clothes.

She leans over and takes my chin in her hands. She kisses my nose, strokes my side. “Don’t tell Cole, little one.”

Chapter Twenty-one

Cole and Elena made the drive out to the Bloomfield estate mostly in silence. Marco put his front feet on the back of Elena's seat and stared out the window. Occasionally he saw something threatening and barked. But mostly he just stood guard. No one else spoke.

Cole figured Elena was just about at the end of her rope. Worried about Javier, sure, but now that he and Shannon had planted the seed that Javier could have killed Donald, was she also terrified that it could be true? Cole was glad he hadn't said anything about his fear that Javier might be dead. But Elena was no fool; she had to suspect the same thing.

Cole turned into the driveway and stopped. The gate stood wide open. Marco crawled from the backseat into Elena's lap.

"What the hell is this?" Cole muttered.

Elena looked at him and shrugged. Marco barked.

"The gate's never been open before." Cole frowned, then drove on. Instead of angling off to the right toward the ten-bay garage next to the main house, Cole angled left onto a one-lane graveled drive that led to Irene's. Cole crept along the drive. He'd never been this way and didn't want to slam the share-car into an unexpected pothole. He braked at a sharp bend. And was glad he did. Reggie Ordway and Krista stood in the middle of the road. Reggie reached out and grabbed her. He pulled her to him. Cole unlatched his seat belt, reached out to open his door.

Krista lifted her face to Reggie's and kissed him. Their bodies entwined in a passionate embrace.

Cole pondered whether to honk the horn. That seemed rude. But so did sitting there watching. The car was hybrid, quiet, so maybe the couple in the road didn't realize anyone watched. It was pretty clear they didn't really care.

Cole and Elena sat quietly. Marco growled.

"It's okay." Cole patted Marco on the side to quiet him. "Weird, but okay." Huh. This was the gold-digger Irene disapproved of. Poor Krista.

Seconds ticked away. How long would it take one of them to come up for air? Voyeurism wasn't his thing. Maybe that's how Ordway felt the evening he'd chased Cole and Christine off the beach. Cole drummed his fingers on the steering wheel until Marco crawled over and licked his fingers.

Elena stared out the window, swiveling her head to take in the garden her brother had rehabilitated. "It's beautiful," she whispered.

Cole shut off the purring engine and leashed up Marco. He patted Elena on the shoulder. "They're expecting us but you don't have to be here if you don't want to."

"I want to." Elena sighed. "As soon as the road block has cleared." She pointed to Ordway and Krista.

Cole opened his door. Marco leapt out, pulled to the end of his leash, and barked at the couple in the road. Krista jumped back, her eyes wild. Reggie rotated slowly.

"Son a bitch." Ordway pushed Krista behind him, then took a step toward Cole. He rested his right hand on the butt of his sidearm. "Get the hell off this property."

"I don't think so." Cole shook his head.

Reggie took another step toward Cole.

Krista reached out and touched Reggie's arm. "Don't."

"Why's the gate open?" Cole pointed back down the drive.

"None of your damn business." Ordway remained rigid, glaring at Cole. "Get out."

Marco growled.

"I apologize for the interruption, Krista. I'm on my way to see your mother." Cole nodded at Krista and went back to the car door. He put one foot in the door and waited.

Krista stepped around Reggie and walked over to Cole. "Please, Mr. Steele. Please don't tell my mother."

Ordway walked up behind her, laid a hand on her shoulder. "It's okay, Krista."

"You do know she already knows about you two, don't you?" Cole waited.

"How?" Krista turned toward Ordway. "How does she know?"

Ordway shook his head, pulling her gently to his side. "Really, it's okay." He stepped onto a path that led away from the drive, drawing her with him. Without a backward glance they walked away.

Cole got back in the car and shut the door. He didn't know where to rank this bizarre encounter in the order of bizarre encounters he'd had with this family. He drove on and parked at Irene's. "You ready?"

Elena nodded and opened her door.

The front door of Irene's cottage opened before Cole knocked. Jackie ushered them into the living room where Irene sat on the couch. A plate of cookies, another of dog treats, and a pot of tea with four cups sat on the coffee table. How did Irene and Jackie know they were coming? And hadn't they had enough tea? Cole sure had and wasn't sure he ever wanted another cup. The repeated tea ritual might be the most bizarre aspect of his visits with Irene.

He introduced Elena to the two women. Irene stood and held out her hand to Elena. "I am so pleased to meet you. Please sit." She bent over and patted Marco. "Hello, precious child." Irene sat again and patted the sofa beside her. Marco jumped up, and Irene unclipped his leash. Jackie sat beside Marco. Elena and Cole each took an overstuffed chair on the other side of the coffee table.

"What can I do for you, Ms. Ortega?" Irene poured a cup of tea and handed it to Elena.

"I want to see my bother." Elena glanced at Cole.

"Ah." Irene poured tea in the remaining cups. "Please help yourself to cookies." She took one of the treats and handed it to Marco. He took it and wagged his tail.

"We haven't seen him yet." Jackie sipped her tea.

Irene glanced at her watch. "He should be here soon."

Elena shifted in her seat. "I'm very worried."

Irene nodded, but didn't say anything.

"I need to understand Javier's role in your scheme." Cole ignored the cookies.

"What scheme is that, Mr. Steele?" Irene sipped.

"Aren't we past that?" Cole sighed. "The one where you, Jackie, Blake, and Brenda stole your husband's money – collected in cash. And somehow coerced Javier to take part."

Irene laughed. A full-throated, deep belly laugh. "Believe me, I did not need to coerce him."

"I don't believe you." Elena's voice cracked. "He's no thief."

"No, but he has a refined sense of justice." Irene set her teacup down. "And he saw the justice in recovering the money that Donald had stolen from Charles Hawkins and your brother, Anthony."

"Yes, we know the botanic garden was simply a ruse to steal money." Cole didn't ask. He and everyone else knew the answer.

"Not exactly." Irene leaned forward. "While it was a ruse to steal money, the goal was to ruin that son-of-a-bitch."

"You said that before, but now that I know you own this estate, there are a few things I don't understand." Cole held up an index finger.

"Only a few, Mr. Steele?" Irene smirked.

"Why collect the money in cash?" Cole ignored the interruption.

"I'm betting you know the answer to that." Irene settled back again.

Cole remained silent, then nodded his head. "Easier to launder."

"Just so."

Cole held up another finger. "Why didn't you just divorce him or retake possession of the estate? Kick him out?"

"You are a nosy bastard, aren't you?" Irene laughed. "No harm in answering now, I suppose. Because we had a pre-nup I couldn't get out of. For some reason the sorry S.O.B. still trusted my financial advice, so I persuaded him to sign over the estate to me to protect it from all the vultures coming after it."

"But you instigated the vultures in the first place." Cole could not keep the wonder out of his voice. It made him sound naïve.

"Just so."

"So, where's the money? And where's Javier?" Cole asked.

Irene and Jackie exchanged looks.

"Please, Mrs. Bloomfield." Elena started to stand.

"Sit, sit, Ms. Ortega." Irene waved her back into her seat.

"I can't speak to where his share of the money is, but I can tell you where mine is." Irene paused. "Las Vegas. Your brother was kind enough to drive it down and drop it off for me. He gave it to a friend of mine."

"Of course." Cole smiled. "Your friend owns a casino, I suppose."

Iren nodded.

"Good way to launder some cash."

"Just so." Irene repeated her new favorite phrase.

"So where is Javier now?"

"Well, actually, he should have been home last night." Jackie frowned. "And here by now."

"What?" Elena stood, began to step over Cole's feet to move closer to Irene.

"Fine. Fine." Irene turned to Jackie. "Could you give Scott a call, find out when Javier left?"

"Gladly." Jackie rose, picked up her cell phone, scrolled though her contact list and dialed. The phone beeped as she put it to her ear. "Hey, Scott." She smiled into the phone. "We're checking on our friend we sent to you." She paused. "Uh huh." She nodded. "Yeah. Told you he was a good kid. Glad you liked him." She paused again. "Listen, he's not back yet. . . . really?" She paused again. "When did he leave?" She drew in her breath. "Yeah. Okay. Okay. Gotta go. Thanks a lot. Talk later."

Jackie set the phone down, looked at Irene. "He dropped the cash with Scott and turned right around. Didn't even stay for dinner."

"Where'd he go then?" Irene's eyebrows rose. "If he headed back here, he should have been home three days ago."

"The day I found Donald," Cole said.

Marco Diary Entry 22

Elena stands in the middle of the room. I jump down from the sofa and trot to her side. She's very upset. I put my paw on her leg. She looks down at me but doesn't pick me up. Then she looks at Cole, then Irene, then Cole again.

"I'm going to find Tony." Elena heads for the front door. I follow her. When she flings it open, I turn back and look at Cole. He's standing up now. I whine. I mean to bark, but everyone is so upset. Elena disappears out the door. I don't know whether to go with her of wait for Cole.

A few seconds pass before he thanks Irene and Jackie - I don't think he means it – and follows Elena and me. That's a relief. I trot at his side as we catch up to Elena. I don't think she knows where Tony is. She's just walking fast down a trail that heads toward the river, then angles away to the right toward the farm.

Cole catches up and overtakes her. I run ahead of both of them. I watch Cole over my shoulder. He points the way. We're going to the barn. I run ahead and find Tony outside the barn loading boxes of asparagus into a big truck. I stop at his feet, sit down, and bark. Just once. I don't want him to run away.

He looks up when Cole and Elena arrive. They stop. Neither of them is out of breath. I think Elena doesn't know what to say. I trot over to her and stand beside her. I want her to know I am on her side. This will give her confidence.

She walks stiff-legged to Tony. Her fists are clenched at her sides. "Javier came home three days ago." She stops talking and leans toward Tony.

He loads the box he's holding into the truck and turns toward her. His eyebrows are all crinkled. "What?"

"You heard me." Elena breathes fast. "You called him. The day he got home."

Tony shakes his head. "Yeah. But I didn't talk to him. I swear."

Cole steps forward and touches Elena on her arm. He angles himself between Elena and Tony. I step between Tony and Cole.

"You found his phone. Where?" Cole's voice is soft. That means he's upset.

Tony takes a step back. "In the garden." He bends his head to one side.

"Show us." Cole steps back and to the side, taking Elena's elbow and bringing her with him. I dance out of the way, so they don't step on me. I don't want to be a tripping hazard.

Tony nods and starts up the path the way we just came. No one says anything, but everyone walks steadily.

I take the lead even though I do not know exactly where we are going. I pick up all the scents I can. So that I can help find where the phone was. I keep an eye on Tony to make sure he takes us to the right spot. I'll smell the phone if it was there. We come to an open, grassy area, where shrubs and flowers are carefully spread out in mounds of dirt covered with bark mulch. We have an area like this at our place. They call these the perennial beds. Tony takes us to a shrub that smells familiar. It smells like the beans that were in that jar. I stop. And bark. I bark and bark. It's dangerous.

Cole squats beside me and stokes my side. "It's okay, Marco, we won't eat it."

Okay, Cole. But I keep a sharp eye on all of them.

Tony kneels down and points to a spot near the base of the shrub. "It was right here."

I push in beside him and bury my nose in the mulch. Yep. He's telling the truth. The phone was here.

Cole stands and looks around. "About half way between the barn and the beach pavilion."

"What does that mean?" Elena's voice is high and tight.

Cole shakes his head. "Not sure it means anything." He's not telling the truth. I can hear it. He thinks it means something but doesn't want to tell Elena that. I think he doesn't want to scare her. Because the barn is where someone tried to kill us.

We four stand quietly now. No one talks, so they must be thinking. I smell that man who was mean to Cole at the gate that morning we found Donald. He's called Ordway. I growl. I don't like that man. I hear his footsteps getting closer. I whirl and run around the corner of some shrubs toward the man. I have to protect Cole and Elena.

He stops when he sees me. Good. He's holding hands with the woman he was kissing earlier. The woman they call Krista. He drops her hand and keeps walking toward me. She follows him. I think he's going to step on me, so I run back to Cole's side. I growl. Ordway and Krista walk around the shrubs and stop.

"Get back to work, Ortega." Ordway tries to growl like I do, but he doesn't do it very well.

"Bite me." Tony laughs.

I wonder if Ordway will. I watch and wait. But he doesn't. He turns instead toward Cole. "We're real tired of your spying."

"Really? Who's we?" Cole smiles, but I know he's not happy.

"The whole family, Mr. Steele." Krista steps in front of Ordway.

"He's family now?" Tony moves away from us.

"Yep. Since about an hour go." Ordway reaches out and lifts Krista's hand in his own. He points to the gold bands on their fingers. Krista squeezes Ordway's hand. She starts to laugh, high and squeaky. It hurts my ears.

"Listen, jackass." Ordway drops Krista's hand and walks toward Tony. "When I say get to work, do it." He hunches his shoulders. "I watch. I know what you and your bother are up to."

Cole puts a hand on Ordway's arm. "And what have they been up to?"

Ordway wheels around to face Cole. "Stealing money. Threatening Mr. Bloomfield. Pilfering equipment. You name it."

"Liar." Elena nearly whispers, but I can hear her. I'm sure Ordway does too, because he turns to glare at her. His face is red.

"Reggie." Krista backs up to Ordway's side. She takes his hand. "Don't start a fight. It's our wedding day. We're picking flowers and leaves for our wedding bouquet."

Ordway's shoulders relax. "Okay, baby. What do you want in it?"

"I love the leaves of this plant. They look like big purple maple leaves, and I love these spiky balls" Krista reaches out and touches the dangerous plant where Tony found Javier's phone.

Ordway slaps her hand away from it. "No. No. Beautiful but deadly."

She jumps back. “Really? Javier chose it, and Daddy loved it.”

Chapter Twenty-two

Cole watched Krista and Ordway continue on through the perennial borders, searching for more flowers. Ordway's voice drifted back as he told Krista the attributes of different flowers, their shelf-life, their meaning in Victorian lore. How'd he know so much?

"Ordway doesn't have horticultural training, does he?" Cole asked.

"It's probably because he followed Javier around all the time. Must have picked up **some** knowledge." Tony sneered, making it sound as if that was impossible.

Ordway turned at the sound of Tony's voice. He pointed two fingers at his eyes, then at Tony.

Tony lifted the middle finger of his left hand and shoved it toward Ordway. Ordway smiled and turned away.

"Guess I'll get back to it." Tony walked back toward the barn.

Cole looked down at Marco, who strained against his leash. He stood rigidly, his nose twitching, the nostrils swiveling in different directions as he stared after Ordway. Elena laughed and knelt beside him. She patted Marco's side.

"Well, I've got a few more questions." Cole helped Elena to her feet. "C'mon."

They walked to the sliding glass door at the back of the main house. Cole knocked. Marco sat to wait. Elena fidgeted, shifting her weight from one foot to the other. Just like her brother, Tony, had the first time Cole met him.

Eventually Blake walked through the kitchen to let them in. As the door slid open a strong breeze flowed out from the house. After they slipped through the door, Blake slammed it into place. As usual, Blake said nothing as he turned and led the way toward the cavernous living room. He kept walking when Cole stopped in the main hallway.

The front door stood wide open. Cole stepped toward it and looked out. Men wearing tool belts unloaded equipment from trucks in the driveway. Saws, work benches, sledge hammers. So that's why the gate was open. Cole turned back and walked into the living room. Elena followed him. Marco was already there, having trotted to the end of his leash as he followed Blake.

The whole family stood in a circle in the center of the empty room. No furniture. No rug. Just a gleaming bare oak floor. Blake and Brenda held hands. As did Ordway and Krista. Portia glowered at the other four. She was hissing again, but Cole couldn't hear her words.

Cole had stopped expecting any real information from this bunch. They were all liars. But circumstances had changed since he and Elena had discovered the castor beans. He had to find out what had happened. He cleared his throat. Portia stopped murmuring and all four of them turned toward him. He didn't introduce Elena. Irene knew her name, but he didn't want the rest of them to know it.

"Sorry to disturb you." Cole struggled to remain civil. "I've got a few more questions."

"Oh, really, Mr. Steele." Portia stepped around the others. "When will you stop badgering us?"

"Let me be clear." Cole stepped forward. "I don't care about you, your family, or your sanity. I am here to help a friend. That's it."

Portia backed away, her cheeks flushed.

"We can't be bothered with you or your friend now," Krista said, uncharacteristically bold. She touched Portia on the shoulder. "We have an announcement to make." She beamed.

Portia turned toward her sister. "Oh, what is it?" she snapped.

Krista stepped back again.

"We just returned from the courthouse. We married a couple of hours ago." Ordway's' announcement seemed more triumphant than joyful.

Stunned silence followed.

"We're hoping to hold a luncheon tomorrow. Look." Krista took the flowers from Ordway and held them out to Portia.

Krista's behavior was odd, even for this bunch.

Portia sneered, tried to grab the flowers, but Krista held on.

"Are you mad? We haven't even buried Papa yet." Portia spoke again in her strange French accent.

"So what? Nobody cares." Krista's voice rose. "Everybody hated him."

Portia slapped her. "Liar. Everyone loved him." Tears formed in Portia's eyes. She straightened, took a white lace handkerchief from a pocket, and dabbed at the tears. "We can't even hold the funeral."

"Why not?" Cole took a chance that she would actually answer him.

"The coroner won't release his body until they are sure about the cause of death." Portia pointed at Cole. "It's all your doing, isn't it?"

Elena gasped. Marco barked. That shut everyone up.

"Why was your father fleeing the country?" Cole stared at Portia.

"What are you talking about?" Brenda glared at Cole.

"Ask your sister. She made the arrangements." Cole gestured toward Portia.

Portia clamped her lips together and shook her head.

Brenda grabbed Portia's elbow. "He's telling the truth, isn't he?" Brenda's head swiveled as she tried to look at everyone at once.

Portia's shoulders slumped. "We were going on holiday. Just the two of us."

"To Uruguay? Not a prime vacation spot. No return scheduled. Good place to launder money, though." Cole kind of enjoyed calling out Portia's lie.

"And he wasn't taking you." Ordway's words rumbled in his chest.

"Don't be ridiculous." Portia flicked her hand at him.

"It's true. He told me to get ready." Krista squeaked. "But I didn't want to go."

"So that's why our furniture is gone, the house about to be demolished." Brenda stepped between her sisters. "Because Dad was leaving."

"No." Irene strode into the room with Jackie in her wake. They advanced toward Portia. "That's my doing."

Cole hadn't seen them come in, and Marco must not have heard or even smelled their arrival.

"You've gotten your eviction notice I presume, Portia." Irene's hard tone filled the room. "I have some renovations to do. As quickly as possible." She glared. "The sooner the better." She turned toward Blake and Brenda. "You two may stay upstairs until the renovations are complete. Krista, you'll stay with Jackie and me."

She walked over to Krista and took the flowers away. "Mr. Ordway, we no longer need your services. We'll mail your final paycheck." She paused. "Get out. Now." The last said quietly.

Ordway and Krista took a step back. No one spoke.

Irene turned toward Jackie. "Would you call the new security man? He has a trespasser to eject."

Krista stepped up to her mother. "I won't stay with you, Mother." She gritted her teeth and took a deep breath. "As I told my father, the only way I'd go anywhere without Reggie is over my dead body." She paused. "Or father's."

Marco Diary Entry 23

Cole and Elena are quiet on our drive home. I don't know why but I do know neither of them is happy. Probably because we still don't know where Javier is. But I am very happy we left that house with all those crazy, mean people. They're angry and bad. I am glad we're going home. It's time for our afternoon run and then dinner. Since Cole and Elena are quiet, I don't need to listen, so I can curl up in the back seat and nap.

Cole parks the car up the street from our house, and I jump out the back and trot up to our gate. I wait for Cole to open it then run around the entire perimeter. I have to check, make sure there were no intruders while we were gone. I don't smell any people, but I do smell birds that have landed in the grass, and a rodent that got through the fence. I better show Elena.

I turn back to find her, but she goes into her little house at the bottom of the garden. She closes the door quietly. Cole walks toward his house. I follow him. I'm glad when he changes into his running clothes. I like to hunt with him. And it gives us both time to think. I have a lot of thinking to do.

He clips the leash to my halter, and we trot across the grass to the back gate. He stops to stretch, so I do too. Then we slip out the back and take the trail up into the forest. The dirt is dry and hard at this time of year, but I can still smell all the other dogs and people that have run here in the past few days. Some were here earlier today. I stop to exchange scents with some of the other dogs. Cole runs in place when I do that. The deeper into the forest we go, the more I smell deer. And squirrel, and rabbit, and bird. I stop suddenly. Coyote has been here too.

But I am not distracted. I can think about Elena and Javier while I hunt. How is Cole going to find Javier? Why won't those people help find him? I still think Irene and Jackie are kind, but I don't know why they are sometimes mean. Maybe they are only kind to dogs. I do know they are liars, and I don't like people who lie. After my family lost me, I ran into a lot of liars. People who say they have cookies, but don't. People who catch me and say they are taking me home, but don't. People who pretend to be kind but aren't. I don't like liars. Irene tells lies. She keeps changing her stories. And I don't think any of the others know how to tell the truth. Even Elena tells lies. She didn't tell Cole about the money in the potting shed. I have to show him.

After a while we turn back to head for home. When we slip in through the back gate Cole unlatches my leash. I need him to follow me to the potting shed. I run in front of him, sit down, and bark.

"We'll get dinner in a bit." He laughs and steps around me.

I run in front of him again. I bark and bark and weave in and around his legs. When he slows down, I stand on my hind legs and paw at his thigh.

He kneels beside me. "C'mon, Marco. I gotta hit the shower before dinner." He stands again and heads for home.

I nip at his socks, and growl. Now he knows I'm serious. I run toward the potting shed, then stop and turn to look at him. He stands with his hands on his hips, his head tilted to one side.

I run to him, circle around him then turn back toward the potting shed. He follows me. When I get to the door, I scratch at it until he opens it. I dart to the back of the room where the potting table stands. I push my nose between the pots that Elena put in front of that big bundle of money. I push harder, and one of the pots tips over. I grab that cloth the bundle is wrapped in and pull as hard as I can. I growl to let Cole know how serious this is. I am not playing.

Cole kneels down, moves the pots out of the way, and pulls the bundle out from under the bench. He grunts as he lifts it onto the potting bench. He unwraps the cloth. He whistles. But not to call me. He knows I am right here.

Chapter Twenty-three

Cole rewrapped the bundle of cash and left it on the bench. He paced to the door and back to the bench. If he confronted Elena now, he'd let his anger loose. And that wasn't fair. How often had Shannon reminded him not to jump to conclusions? And anger felt wrong. He'd become intimate with anger over the past year, kept it close ever since Christine's death, used it to blot out anything else he might feel. He took a deep breath. Maybe what he really felt was dismay, confusion.

He stopped marching back and forth. Marco stood on his hind legs and tapped him on the knee. Cole squatted and ruffled the dog's ears. "Yeah. I gotta talk to her. But without anger. You're right."

Maybe Marco had actually meant – "It's dinner time, you know." But Cole chose to believe otherwise.

He debated whether to leave the money where it was. After all, it likely belonged to Javier. Irene had mentioned that he took his share. But Cole thought that meant he'd taken it to Vegas. Apparently not. On the other hand, Nicholas and Shannon deserved to know. They'd both gone out of their way to help. Especially Shannon. Keeping them in the dark didn't seem fair. And, it'd be better if all four of them talked about this new wrinkle. Together.

The bundle of cash was heavy. Really heavy. After ten feet, he turned back and dumped it into a wheelbarrow. He wheeled it to the door of the communal kitchen, hoisted it out of the barrow, and man-handled it through the door. He dropped it just inside and dragged it across the floor.

Marco had preceded Cole through, using the dog door, and already sat at attention on his kitchen pillow. He kept a close eye on Nicholas.

Cole left the bundle on the floor and sat beside Shannon on one of the benches around the long table. Shannon raised an eyebrow then cocked her head toward the bundle.

"Stacks of hundred-dollar bills." Cole sighed. "Elena had them under the potting bench."

Shannon sighed. "Damn."

"Looks like quite a haul." Nicholas laughed.

"You ought to know." Shannon laughed with him.

Nicholas had some experience toting around bales of money from his days as a mule in Mexico. He and Shannon had decided to pay back student loans by helping move cannabis north and money south. They'd thought it'd be easy. Turned out to be the hard way to get out of debt. Nicholas had done a short stretch in prison. He was lucky that Shannon had gone to law school. They'd never crossed that particular line again.

"What do we do about it?" Shannon asked.

"We wait to see what Elena has to say." Cole shrugged.

Nicholas went back to prepping food for dinner, shucking oysters from Netarts Bay.

"So, where do we stand?" Shannon wiped the table, then laid out her notes, a blank pad, and some pens.

Cole told her what had happened at the estate.

"I gotta get my head around this." Shannon restacked and tidied her notes. "Krista and Ordway got married." She wrote that down. "And Irene is tossing Portia out and laying down the law with them all."

"That's about it." Cole chuckled. "Sorry, it's not funny. It just strikes me as so bizarre. I can't tell you how much I'd rather have never met any of these people."

"But you met the family some time ago." Shannon's pen poised over her note pad.

"True." Cole nodded. "But I'm glad to admit I didn't know them very well." He dropped his chin on his hand. "And I was certainly wrong about all of them, especially Donald. I thought they were okay, that Donald was simply the scion of a wealthy family. That he gave a lot of money to charity. I thought Portia was an uptight busy-body. But harmless. And the other daughters merely shy and retiring." He lifted one shoulder. The uninjured one. "And I thought Donald's wife was dead."

"Boy, were you wrong." Nicholas slapped Cole on the back and set a platter of raw oysters with a mignonette sauce on the table.

"Yeah. Irene is anything but." Cole snorted.

Nicholas opened a chilled bottle of a Willamette Valley Pinot Gris and poured out three glasses. No one spoke as they sipped their wine.

"Your twenty-four hours are up." Shannon twirled her glass by the stem between thumb and index finger. "We gotta call the cops."

Cole shook his head. "We need more information. What about the money?" He hooked his thumb toward the bundle by the door.

"That looks pretty bad, Cole."

"I know. But we don't want to cause Elena more grief." Cole slid an oyster into his mouth, chewed and swallowed. "If the coroner doesn't suspect murder, how can we justify stirring up more trouble for Elena?"

Shannon frowned. "The coroner would never reach a conclusion without specific evidence, but he must at least suspect something. Otherwise he would have released Donald's body." She wrinkled her brow. "I'm an officer of the court, Cole. I cannot withhold information." Marco trotted over to her and jumped up beside her. He rested his head on her arm and stared up into her face. She smiled. "Let me call Suzy." She took out her cell. "The assistant coroner."

"Who don't you know?" Cole took a sip of wine.

Shannon got hold of her friend, and after a bit of catching up, asked the question on her mind. "Is Mr. Bloomfield's condition consistent with ricin poisoning?" Shannon listened and nodded. "Thanks, Suzy. Yeah. I'll let you know as soon as I can." Shannon stabbed the off button and laid her phone on the table. "As we already know the poison in castor beans is ricin, and that ricin is undetectable. Suzy thinks that would explain everything."

"Shit." Nicholas sat heavily beside Shannon.

"Yeah." Shannon rubbed her forehead. "Didn't you take photos?" She turned to Cole. "The morning that you found Donald."

Cole nodded.

"Let's see them." Shannon cleared her notes out of the way.

Cole took out his phone, leaned it horizontally against the wine bottle, already close to empty. He opened the gallery app and found the first image of that beach scene. He and Shannon put their heads together and looked at the screen. Nicholas walked over and stood behind them.

Cole had forgotten how many photos he'd taken and how many details he'd captured. It hadn't seemed important until they discovered the castor beans. But even then, it was a tenuous connection, and there was no reason to suspect murder. Javier was the head gardener. Of course he'd have seeds from a plant on the estate. But why had he carried around those and no others?

The images came up in the order he'd taken them. An overview of the beach, tall grasses growing along the sandy shoreline. A clearing where the pavilion stood off to the right. Four by four timbers held up the translucent roof. Along one side, where an exterior wall might have been, ran a kitchen counter. Dark walnut cabinets, a stainless-steel counter top with a deep sink in the middle. To the left of the sink stood an elaborate coffee-making station – a coffee grinder, an espresso machine, a milk steamer. Above that on glass shelves jars of different kinds of beans. Each jar was labeled, but the labels were too far away to read.

The next image was closer. A square, glass-topped, ebony table with two straight-back chairs stood in the center of the sandy clearing. Grasses surrounded the clearing. Donald's body, wrapped in the tablecloth, where Cole had left him, wasn't visible in the shot.

Shannon grunted then slid her finger across the screen to reveal the next photo. This one was close on Donald's inert form, the pool of blood next to his head had not yet soaked completely into the sand. Shannon pointed to the slight discoloration on Donald's forehead.

Cole shook his head. "I didn't notice that at the time." He flicked the image away. The center of the clearing with the table, two chairs drawn up to it appeared on screen. "The chairs must have been moved."

"By whom? And when?"

Cole shrugged and swiped across the screen, revealing the glass table top with one full cup of coffee, one empty.

Shannon flipped to the next image. A close-up of the sole of Donald's shoe, smooth and shiny. Then footprints in the sand. Despite the soft surface one set of prints were clearly Donald's, another set quite different. Larger and with a waffle pattern. Barely discernible in the soft sand, yet distinct from the smooth soles of Donald's shoes.

"So, Donald did meet with someone." Cole spoke softly.

"Doesn't mean it was Javier." Shannon tapped to the next photo. Another picture of footprints. Several more pictures followed. Some of faint depressions in the sand, others were elongated and scuffled.

"Almost looks like a fight." Cole ran his finger across the screen again. More of the same. "Shit. How did I miss that?"

The next image came up. Near the edge of the clearing where grasses skirted one side - a depression in the sand made the vague outline of a human body. Cole held his breath. In the next picture – broken and trampled grass where the grasses separated the clearing from the expanse of beach that led to the river.

"How I spent my summer vacation." Nicholas grunted above Cole's head.

"I don't get it." Shannon moved to the last image: Deep footprints – the waffled-soled boots – led away from the grass toward the river's edge.

"Someone left Donald there to die," Cole said.

Marco Diary Entry 24

I sit at my place at the table next to Shannon while Nicholas makes a delicious dinner. He gives me one oyster. Cold and salty, it slithers around in my mouth. It tastes like the ocean. Nicholas puts a plate of meat – the kind they call foie gras – in front of me. When Cole says okay, I eat it in one bite. Sometimes they tell me to slow down and savor the food. I wonder if they have ever been starving like I was. After that I get a plate of roasted vegetables. They're delicious, but not as good as the meat.

Elena does not join us for dinner. The bundle of money sits on the floor. While we eat no one talks about it, or Javier, or our troubles. I am happy for that. Because when they talk about Cole and my investigation everyone gets sad. Instead we talk about when we're going to the beach, then the new exhibit at the art museum. They change the subject again and talk about a concert they want to go to. I'll go too. I like music.

Nicholas gives me some sliced apples and a little piece of cake for dessert. After that I go outside for my evening patrol. I check every scent left behind today while we were at the estate. I smell no strangers. That's good.

Cole and I go to bed early. I sleep pretty well, but I hear Cole tossing and turning. Every time he thrashes around in his bed, I sit up to listen and sniff. I growl in case bad guys are coming. But I never hear or smell any. I think they are in his dreams. So, I go back to sleep until the next time Cole turns over to slap his pillow into shape.

I am not too tired in the morning because I take short naps. That's the only way to sleep safely when you are on the run, like I was after my first family lost me.

When it's time to get up I kiss Cole's face. That's the best way to start a new day. With brand new kisses. He smiles and takes my face in his hands. "Good morning, Marco." He smells like he hasn't slept well, which I already know. I also know my kisses will help give him energy.

After coffee, which I don't drink, and breakfast, which is dry dog food for me, and then our morning run, Cole drives us back out to Irene's house. I don't want to visit these people anymore, but I know we still need to help Elena.

When we arrive Irene and Jackie are sitting on their couch. I wonder if they ever sit anywhere else. I wonder if they already know we are coming. They offer no tea. Or cookies. I say hello anyway, to be polite. Then go sit beside Cole and lean against his leg.

"I'm sorry you've come all this way. But we can't imagine where Javier is." Jackie is telling the truth. Her voice is calm, her eyes clear, and she smells the way she always does when she's not angry.

"I wish we did know where he is." Irene blinks and her voice shakes. "I'm worried sick." I don't know whether she tells the truth or whether her worry makes her sound so different. She smells different too.

Cole sighs. I feel how uncertain he is. "We've uncovered some terrible information. I thought you should know about it."

Irene looks at him but doesn't speak. I smell her agitation.

"We think Donald may have been poisoned." Cole takes his cell phone from his pocket. No one speaks.

He pushes several buttons then hands the phone to Irene. She sits with her hands folded in her lap. Jackie leans over and takes the phone.

"What am I looking at?" Jackie sets the phone down on the coffee table.

"Footprints walking away from Donald's body. Left on the beach before I arrived."

Everyone is quiet. And very tense. It makes me nervous. But I wait quietly just as Cole does.

"Yes, Mr. Steele." Irene nods, then leans back. "I killed that son of a bitch."

Jackie gasps and reaches over to take Irene's hand. "Don't"

"He got what he deserves." Irene pats Jackie's hand. "I have no regrets."

Everyone sits like statues. I raise my head and sniff. It smells like a storm. The air around them is wavy and charged with energy. It scares me. I lean harder against Cole's leg. He pats the side of my neck.

"I don't believe you." Cole's voice is so quiet I am not sure anyone can hear him but me.

"Believe what you want." Irene shrugs and looks away. She is lying.

"It makes no sense. You could have divorced him, thrown him out, or simply ruined him as you planned." Cole jiggles his leg up and down. Not the one I lean against, but I still feel his agitation and how hard he tries to contain it.

"You must see that I have the best motive in the world." Irene waves her hand like she's shooing a fly away.

"There are plenty of motives to go around." Cole keeps his voice low.

"But I gain everything with him out of the way. The estate all to myself without having to share it with that despicable cow. I get my children back. I get my home back." Irene is nearly shouting. Her lower lip trembles.

Cole shakes his head. "Sorry. I don't buy it." He stares at her for a minute. "Who are you protecting?"

Chapter Twenty-four

Irene let go of Jackie's hand and stood. "We're done here, Mr. Steele. See yourself out." She walked out of the room alone.

Jackie stood. "I am truly sorry, Mr. Steele. There's nothing more to say."

"Sure, there is. Where's Javier?"

"I have no idea." She walked to the front door and opened it.

Marco jumped up and trotted toward the open door until he reached the end of his leash. Cole stood and walked out the door. It closed softly behind them. What more could he do? He finally agreed with Shannon. He had to call the police. He'd do it as soon as he got home.

Cole turned toward the parked car, but Marco pulled on the leash and trotted down a path that led toward the beach. The overgrown path that Marco had tried to show him the first day they came here. It led to the beach pavilion. To the secluded clearing in the sand where Donald had spent his last hours before his trip to the hospital. Irene could easily have sneaked down here early that morning. It couldn't hurt to take another look. So he let Marco lead him toward the river.

He walked slowly despite Marco's anxious pull on the leash. He pondered Irene's confession. Was she protecting one of her daughters? There didn't seem to be anyone else she cared about. Except, maybe Jackie. But what in the world would drive Jackie to concoct a devious plan to poison Donald? Irene was the devious one. Certainly, the most devious person Cole had met during this entire escapade. Maybe in his whole life.

Cole shook his head as he walked. All he'd managed to uncover was what an awful human being Donald Bloomfield had been. The man had lied, cheated, stolen, and ruined other peoples' lives, including those of his own daughters. A real snake in the grass, as Cole's mother used to say. Maybe Irene was right. Good riddance.

But he'd utterly failed Elena. Given all his intrusive questioning, his meddling, his repeated trips to this estate, he'd managed to uncover nothing about Javier's whereabouts. Sure, he'd discovered Irene's plot to ruin Donald, to recover the money he'd stolen from Blake, Brenda, Charley, and Tony. Cole had also discovered that Irene had entangled Javier in her machinations. And that he'd come away with about a million dollars as a result. But none of this helped Elena.

Marco ran ahead and disappeared over the small grass-covered dune that blocked his view of the beach pavilion. Cole slogged through the soft sand, not certain he wanted to go back to this spot. Certain he didn't actually.

But since he and Marco were there he might as well take another look. He'd missed so much when he took those pictures, he needed to look again. He topped the rise and stopped. He scanned the scene. Marco stood on his hind legs and pawed at Cole's knees.

The square table sat in the center of the clearing. Its two dark matching chairs sat at right angles to the table top. As he expected, the tablecloth in which he'd wrapped Donald was gone. The sand in the clearing had been raked and smoothed. Even the red spot where Donald's blood had soaked into the sand was gone. Who had cleaned it up?

He walked slowly down the short slope and over to the kitchen counter. The cabinet doors he'd left open were shut, the countertop and sink sparkling clean. The shelves still stood to the left of the sink, but the coffee grinder, the coffee maker, and jars of beans were gone.

Marco barked, tugged on the leash, nearly pulling it from Cole's hand. The pup dug his feet into the sand, kept pulling, jack-rabbiting in place. Cole followed slowly. They crossed the clearing to the edge where the grasses grew tall. The ones that had appeared broken and trampled in the photos he'd taken were neatly trimmed. The sand beyond the grasses was swept smooth. No footprints remained.

Marco bounded over the grasses, pulling and barking. Cole leaned over and unclipped the leash.

Marco Diary Entry 25

I'm running. My nose to the ground. Snuffing up sand and bits of grass and sea shells. I stop to sneeze. Then pressing my nose into the sand, I look for the scent. I lose it for a minute. So I circle around, pick it up again. I run to the water's edge.

The scent vanishes. I run along the line where water washes back and forth almost erasing the smell I must follow. I run as fast as I can while the water moves, nearly washing away what I need to find. I look back to make sure Cole is following me. I know he can't keep up, but I want to make sure he is coming. He is.

I turn back to the task, searching everywhere with my nose. I smell what I am looking for again. The faint scent takes me down the beach further away from the clearing where that man was dying. Now the smell is stronger. I keep running.

It's really strong now. And then I run past it. I turn back. And bark. Cole is coming. I start digging. I dig as fast as I can.

Cole runs to my side. He watches. Then starts digging too. He scoops up sand with his hands. I dig even faster. Pretty soon we have a hole about two feet deep. It's too deep for me to get to the bottom. Cole picks me up and puts me down beside the hole. He keeps digging.

Then he stops. I look over the side of the hole and see a man's hand. I jump down into the hole and sniff the hand. It's Javier. I growl.

Cole leans forward, resting on his hands on either side of the hole. "Damn," he says. He wipes his hands, takes out his phone, and makes a call.

Chapter Twenty-five

Cole clipped Marco's leash to his halter and dragged him away from his project to dig up Javier. Marco gave up easily and walked with Cole down the beach, upriver, away from the farm, the barn, and the big house. Though he couldn't see it, Irene's cottage hunkered to his left, the river flowing to his right.

Maybe his first instinct about Irene had been right, that she ruled over a family cartel of sorts. That she controlled a criminal conspiracy in which her daughters and son-in-law participated. He swore under his breath. Marco looked up at him. The dog's eyebrows drew together, his ears pricked up. He stopped in front of Cole and stood on his hind legs, pawing at Cole's knees. Cole squatted and stroked the pup's sides.

"Don't worry." Cole sat in the sand.

Marco crawled into Cole's lap and licked his face, then circled a few times and settled with one front leg hitched over Cole's knee. Cole stared at the flowing river. Marco stared at Cole.

Cole and Christine had been here just a few weeks before she died. He'd cherished memories of that night at the fund-raiser. Now they were tainted. Not ruined, perhaps, but colored by more death, by Elena's distress. How could he fix that? Did he even want to? He closed his eyes.

Marco shoved his nose under Cole's hand, reminding Cole that love persisted. Despite Christine's absence.

Cole opened his eyes, leaned forward with a groan. He'd been sleep-walking for a year. He definitely needed to fix that.

"I should have done something sooner." Cole slapped the ground. "I could have stopped this."

Marco raised his head and growled. He lept from Cole's lap, wagging his tail. He ran to the end of his leash until he could go no further. He strained against the leash and barked.

Cole turned to see what caught the dog's attention. Shannon walked toward them. She'd made a wide berth around Marco's hole at the river's edge, approaching them from the trail that led to Irene's.

Cole stood and walked toward Shannon. Marco ran to her, jumped up, wagging his tail and turning in circles to greet her. The three met some hundred yards upriver from the beach clearing.

"Cole." Shannon enveloped him in a hug.

"I know." Cole stood with his arms at his sides.

Shannon leaned back, holding Cole at arm's length. "This is not your fault." She glowered at him.

"I'm going to get the son, or daughter-of-a-bitch who did this." Cole took a step back. "Don't tell me I can't."

Shannon shook her head. "Not about to."

"I don't give a damn for the legal niceties." Cole paced toward the river bank and back. "Where are the cops?"

"On their way."

"How'd you beat them here?" Cole started back toward the beach pavilion.

"I didn't call them until I got here." Shannon twisted around to watch Cole walk away.

"What?" Cole stopped.

"I wanted to be here first. They're not going to be happy that you keep finding bodies on the beach. In the same place."

"You think I need a lawyer?" Cole laughed.

"Can't hurt." Shannon joined Cole by the river. "Where's the family?"

"I don't know. I left Irene and Jackie at Irene's. Haven't seen the others." Cole walked toward the path that led to Irene's.

"You need to stick around, Cole."

He nodded then stood still, looking down at the sand. "Two murders in the same spot." He turned toward Shannon. "We need to know when Javier died. Can you keep in touch with Suzy at the coroner's office? Find out what you can?"

"Of course." Shannon nodded.

"Let's assume Donald told the truth. That he met Javier for coffee. Three days ago, now." Cole began pacing again, but this time in a tight circle. "That was the same morning I stood outside the gate. Waiting for someone to open it."

"Who'd want them both dead?" Shannon stood still watching Cole circle.

"That's a good question." Cole stopped. "Donald was dying while I waited at the gate. Was Javier dying too?"

Marco put his nose in the air. His ears pricked, and he sniffed. Then Cole heard the sirens. He bent down and ruffled Marco's ears. "We're going to be here awhile. Sorry, little fella."

Marco licked Cole's face.

Marco Diary Entry 26

The siren stops. I'm glad because it hurts my ears. Policemen come down the path and talk to Cole and Shannon. They try to take me away from Cole and make me stand by the police cars. But Cole won't let go of my leash. They string up yellow tape, put white fabric around the hole I dug. When they start to take Cole away, he hands my leash to Shannon. I bark and bark. Shannon and I follow.

"I'm Mr. Steele's attorney," Shannon says when we get to the police car. She has her serious face on. "He won't answer any questions without me present."

We stand around beside one of the cars, and two policemen ask lots and lots of questions. They ask some good ones about when and how we found Javier. Do we know who we found? How do we know who it is? Cole says he can't be sure because he never met Javier. But I know who it is.

They also ask some stupid questions, like how does Cole know Javier, even though Cole has already told them they never met. I stop listening because I have to think. If Cole is right, and Javier saw Donald that first morning we came here, and if Donald drank those beans I found and later died, then someone in the family killed them both.

I don't think about why. Even though I know Cole wants to know why. I never understand why people do mean things. And this is really mean. Mostly I think about what Cole and I can do for Elena. We need to find out who killed her brother. I want to go home and see her. I want to crawl into her lap and make her feel better. She will be very sad.

"Here's my card." Shannon's voice is sharp. "Call for an appointment. Mr. Steele will make himself available." She hands something to a detective and takes Cole by the elbow.

Cole shakes her hand off his arm. He takes my leash from her. We walk to our car and Shannon walks to hers. Before he opens the door, Cole turns to her. "I really don't think that was necessary."

"I suspect you're right, but it's time – way past time – to disentangle ourselves from the damaged family drama." Shannon opens her car door. "Let's talk at home."

I sit in the front seat with my front legs propped on the dashboard. Cole doesn't like it when I do that, he says I could get hurt. But I keep my balance. I pay attention. And today he's distracted and doesn't say anything.

At home Cole and Shannon disappear into the kitchen. I go find Elena. She needs me. She's in the vegetable garden, weeding. She's working hard and is all sweaty. I lick her arms and legs, then help her dig weeds. I'm very good at it.

The sun gets hotter and I wonder when Elena will want to quit. It's almost lunch time. But I can feel her fear and I don't want to make her hurry. It will break her heart when Cole tells her about Javier. I know about losing your family. I'll wait here with her and help her pull weeds until Cole comes.

When he finally does, Elena stiffens and turns her face away. I run to her and lick her face. Cole kneels beside her. Shannon and Nicholas cross the grass to sit on Elena's other side. I crawl into her lap.

"We found Javier." Cole speaks softly. He tells her the whole story.

Elena barely reacts, but I feel her heart breaking. I lean against her. We sit in silence for a long time.

"I knew it." Elena's eyes fill with tears. "He would have called me." She leans over and buries her face in my hair. She sobs. No one else speaks. But they all rest their hands on Elena's back and arms.

We stay still until Nicholas gets up into a crouch. He takes Elena and me into his arms and carries us into the kitchen. Cole and Shannon follow. Nicholas puts us down on one of the benches. I crawl from her lap and sit beside her. The others sit on the bench beside us. Everyone is sad. And no one talks.

Elena straightens her back and looks at each of us. "I want to know what happened." Her voice is steady and hard.

"You got it." Cole's tone matches Elena's. He walks over to the computer desk and picks up Shannon's yellow pad of notes. I sit very still beside Elena and listen. Cole flips through the pages. "Okay. What do we know?"

"Irene married Donald thirty years ago when she was at the height of her career as a porn star. Despite leaving him twenty years ago, she remained on the estate and actually owns the entire property." Shannon does not look at any notes. "An estate that has been in the Bloomfield family for a hundred years."

"You'd think that would give someone a really good motive to kill Irene, not Donald." Nicholas speaks softly. He never does that.

"We know Portia is Donald's step-daughter and has always hated Irene." Cole flips a page on the pad.

"You're making my point, brother." Nicholas chuckles then clears his throat.

"Okay, let's speed this up." Shannon takes the pad from Cole. She lifts one finger at a time as she speaks. "Donald put Charley, Blake, and Ordway out of business three years ago."

"Despite the fact that Blake is married to one of his daughters," Cole says.

"Maybe because of it." Shannon keeps talking. "All three of them accepted positions from Donald to work at the estate. Why?"

"I'm assuming they all got offers they couldn't refuse." Cole begins to pace. That's what he does when he's thinking. Not me. I sit very still, or sometimes I lie down and rest my chin on my paws. "I suspect the offers they couldn't refuse came from Irene. Although they all have plausible stories about why they came to work for Donald."

"That's beginning to make sense." Shannon nods. "That's when she hatched her plan to ruin Donald and get everyone's money back in the process."

"Except for Ordway." Cole stops pacing. "She didn't include him in the plan."

"But she included Javier, a man she barely knew." Shannon cocks her head to one side. "So she'd have a scapegoat?"

"Seems likely." Cole holds up a hand. "But I'm trying to follow your counsel by not jumping to conclusions. As creditors, and possibly the FBI, started closing in, Donald made plans to flee the country."

"With Krista." Shannon shakes her head, her voice high and tight.

Everyone is quiet now. I lay my chin in Elena's lap. I'm thinking.

"I still got questions." Nicholas squares his shoulders. "Who put the beans in Donald's special coffee blend? Who locked Cole and Marco in the barn and started the fire? And why? Why did Irene confess to killing Donald? And who the hell killed Javier?"

I raise my head and bark. I know. But how do I tell Cole?"

Chapter Twenty-six

Cole turned to Shannon. "Would you call your friend at the coroner? We need to know when Javier died." He glanced at Elena. "And what killed him."

Shannon picked up her phone and dialed while Cole walked over to the fridge and opened the door. "What can you put together for a quick lunch?"

Nicholas rose and grabbed a loaf of Dakota bread. He slapped it on the counter and began to slice it. He took some Brie from a cupboard, some steak from the fridge, and began making sandwiches. Marco jumped down, trotted over to his bed, and watched Nicholas work. Cole poured out some iced tea for everyone and put the glasses on the table.

"Thanks, Suzy. I appreciate it." Shannon set her phone down, looking from Cole to Elena. "You okay, Elena? You want to hear this?"

Elena nodded.

So did Shannon. "These are preliminary results, of course. But it looks like he died the morning you found Donald on the beach." Shannon looked at Cole. "Of blunt force trauma. Appears he got hit on the back of the head with something flat. A shovel maybe."

Cole nodded slowly, holding a glass of tea half-way to his mouth. He closed his eyes, conjuring what he'd seen the morning he found Donald. Recalling the photos he'd taken that day, picturing the cleaned-up site he'd looked at this morning. "We have to get these photos to the police." Cole handed Shannon his phone. "Would you download them to a flash drive? Then file-share them to the detective in charge?"

Shannon took the phone and got to work at the computer.

"Wait. Wait." Cole walked up behind her. "Look at those of the footprints again. That waffle pattern." The photos stopped fluttering across the screen. Shannon scrolled through them slowly. "There." Cole pointed. "That's it." He picked up Shannon's phone and handed it to her. "Would you call Suzy back? Ask her about the soles of Javier's shoes."

Shannon stepped away and called again, while Cole distributed the sandwiches around the table. He tipped some dry dog food into a small dish and set it at Marco's place. Marco jumped up and sniffed the bowl, then looked at Cole's sandwich with hurt in his eyes. "Sorry little rascal. You'll get something special tonight."

Marco sat and tilted his head toward Cole.

"Okay." Cole nodded.

Marco ate with little enthusiasm. When he finished, he stretched his neck out and gave Cole's sandwich another sniff.

Shannon walked back toward the table and disconnected her call. She leaned on the table, looking at Cole. "Nope. Javier wore sneakers, not boots. No waffle pattern." She restarted the photo download to the file-share site. "Needless to say, Suzy is eager to get her hands on these images."

"Alrighty then." Cole grabbed his sandwich and headed for the door. Marco jumped down and followed. Cole grabbed Marco's leash and they both trotted to the share-car parked up the street.

Marco jumped into the front seat and refused to get in the back. Cole let it go. He drove one-handed while he scarfed down his sandwich, headed again to the estate on Sauvie Island.

When they got there, the gate was wide open again. He drove as close to the ten-bay garage as he could get. The gravel drive and stone-paved parking area were full of panel vans and pick-up trucks packed with equipment. The family cars must have all been parked inside the garage, out of sight. Not accessible. Good. They couldn't take off until he had some answers.

Cole opened his door and got out of the car. He turned to clip Marco's leash to his halter, but Marco slipped by and danced out of reach. "Okay, shrimp. But you listen and do what I say."

Cole shut the car door and turned toward the house. Marco slid by and ran to the front door of the mansion. It stood open, and Marco trotted right in. Cole caught up to him in the entry. The long red Persian runner was gone. Thick paper meant to protect the wood floors lay in its place. Construction dust hovered in the air. The walls were bare. Deeper within the house saws buzzed and sledge hammers slammed.

Maybe the family cars weren't in sight because they'd all left during the demolition phase of the remodel. Cole was curious what Irene would do. Anything would be better than the gold-leaf mantel and gaudy chandelier. Curiosity raised, he peered into the cavernous living room. Nothing remained of its former garish glory.

Back in the hallway Marco stood alert at the bottom of the staircase, waiting for Cole. The pup barked, started up the stairs, and then waited for Cole to follow. They climbed the stairs together.

They found the family in the sitting room at the top of the stairs. Here the furniture remained. In fact, except for the wreckage of the missing portraits – which had all been carted away – this part of the house appeared untouched.

Irene and Jackie sat on the leather couch. Blake sat in the club chair closest to the windows, Brenda in the other. The glass coffee table was bare, except for a game console on the shelf beneath.

Ordway and Krista stood in front of the blank 75-inch flat screen, while Portia hovered beside the open casement window. All of them stared grimly as Cole and Marco stopped at the top of the stairs. The air crackled with silent emotion. Marco growled and sat. Cole stood beside Marco.

"You again." Ordway sniped.

"We're in the middle of something here, Mr. Steele. This conversation is private," Irene said with uncharacteristic hesitancy.

"Carry on." Cole bowed and gestured for them to continue, as though he were their magnanimous host rather than the nosy interloper. With Marco at his side, Cole crossed the room and stood behind the sofa across from Ordway and Krista.

"I had every reason to want that bastard dead." Irene's voice shook.

"Perhaps. But you didn't kill him. And everyone here knows that." Cole looked at Ordway. "The morning I arrived for my appointment with Donald, why didn't you open the gate or respond to the intercom?"

Ordway squared his shoulders. "I don't answer to you, Steele."

"For Christ's sake, Reggie, answer the man." Blake spoke through clenched teeth.

"I was busy." Ordway leaned toward Blake. "And I don't answer to you either."

"In fact, you do." Blake stood, but made no move toward Ordway. "Obviously you were too busy to do your job. What were you too busy doing?"

Cole rolled his eyes at the pissing contest.

"He was with me." Krista laid a hand on Ordway's arm.

"Nonsense." Irene snapped. "You were shopping with me."

"No more lies, Mama. No more secrets." Krista lifted her chin. "I love Reggie and he loves me."

"Nonsense." Irene repeated.

"Stop it. Both of you." Cole stepped around the end of the sofa, stopping by the club chair where Brenda sat. "Someone did finally open the gate, and you, Krista were in the living room with your sisters."

"Just as I thought." Irene's voice rose. "You're a good girl, Krista."

"I'm not a girl, Mama, good or bad. And now I'm a married woman." Krista walked to the coffee table and loomed over her mother. "And don't say nonsense."

Marco trotted to her and sniffed Krista's feet. He circled her, huffing up scents from her shoes. He looked up at Cole.

"Who opened the gate for me?"

"I did." Blake sat down again.

Cole nodded. Made sense. "Why do you think your mother claims to have killed your father?" Cole looked at Brenda, then Krista.

"Maybe she did." Brenda leaned back in her chair, meeting Cole's gaze.

"Nonsense." Cole smiled. "As your mother would say."

Marco trotted to Brenda. He circled her, sniffing at her shoes, as he had done to Krista. Again, he looked up at Cole.

"If Irene killed Donald, why kill Javier?" Cole didn't move. They might balk at his questions any minute.

"Who said she did?" Blake scowled at Cole.

Cole ignored the question. "Describe Donald's morning coffee routine."

Blake shrugged. "That's what he did every morning in summer. Got out to the beach about six every day. Ground his own beans, put his special blend du jour in that thousand-dollar espresso machine."

Cole nodded. "Where'd he get the blend he was using the last week?"

"Who knows?" Brenda said. "What's that got to do with anything?'

"Someone here knows the answer to that." Cole glanced at Irene. "Who cleaned up the beach pavilion after Donald died?"

"Really, Mr. Steele." Irene's voice was high and tight. "Some member of the staff, no doubt."

"Don't be ridiculous, Mama." Krista turned toward her mother. "There was no staff. You'd fired everyone." She turned back to Cole. "I cleaned it all up. We couldn't bear to see it that way, could we Reggie? It was simply too sad."

This made no sense. They all hated the man. Marco trotted around the coffee table smelling Jackie's, Irene's, and finally Blake's shoes. He ran his nose along the edge of each sole, over the toes, and up the ankles, looking intently at

Cole after each thorough investigation. What was Marco up to?

Irene stood. "You are not welcome here, Mr. Steele. I really must ask you to leave." She smoothed her skirt. "I'm surrendering myself to the police tomorrow. And we are all dealing with how to proceed."

Cole remained by Brenda's chair. "You didn't kill Donald or Javier, Irene. The police will figure that out soon enough. And you'll be charged with obstructing a police investigation. So sit down and shut up."

Irene paled, but sat down, her hands clenched in her lap. Marco trotted to her and licked her fingers. He crossed the room and sniffed Ordway's boots. Ordway skittered away from him. Marco growled, tail stiff. He stalked toward Ordway again, gave one sharp bark, and looked at Cole.

"Here's what happened." Cole circled around to keep the coffee table between him and the family yet blocking their access to the stairs. "On the morning I arrived for my appointment, Donald met with Javier at the beach pavilion." Cole faced Irene. "Just as he said."

Marco eased away from Ordway and trotted back to Cole's side.

"Someone here put castor beans in Donald's coffee blend." Cole paused. The faces he scanned were blank. "It takes the accumulation of toxins from the beans three days to kill." Silence.

Cole continued. "Whoever prepared that blend had been doing so for three days. Someone with patience. The morning I arrived to talk to Donald, that person, knowing the three days were up, waited nearby. Javier's presence took them by surprise." He paused again. Still no remorse.

"Javier noticed that the coffee tasted off. He told Donald something was wrong. Donald told me Javier got up to check the beans. Someone pushed Donald down, and he hit his head. I saw the red patch on his forehead where he hit the table."

"Yes, exactly." Irene cried. "I put the castor beans in the coffee. I watched Donald meet Javier at the pavilion. I can see it from the path that leads to my house. When Javier noticed the bad coffee, I ran. I pushed Donald down." Irene trembled. Jackie reached over and covered Irene's hands with hers.

"And I suppose you cracked Javier's skull, dragged him up the beach, and buried him." Cole's voice filled with scorn.

"Good riddance." Ordway stepped up beside Krista, still standing in front of the coffee table. He put his arm around her shoulders.

"I didn't do it for you." Irene snarled.

"We all hated the son-of-a-bitch." Ordway's face reddened. "Do you know he planned to take my sweet Krista away?"

"Yes." Irene shouted. "And I stopped him."

"No." Cole shouted over them. "You did not. And neither did Krista. So, you can stop protecting her and tell the truth."

Marco sneaked up behind Ordway. He sniffed the heel of Ordway's boots. He growled, nipping at the boots. Ordway turned and kicked. Marco yelped as the waffle-soled boot connected with his side and sent him flying across the room. He lay still.

Cole leapt over the coffee table and smashed a fist in Ordway's face. Ordway stumbled against the flat screen. It wobbled. Ordway scrambled to regain his footing.

Ordway punched Cole in the gut, knocking the air from his lungs. Cole went down, stayed down, gasping for air.

Marco struggled to his feet and ran across the room. He bit into Ordway's calf. Ordway shook him off and ran for the stairs.

Cole rose. Launched himself at Ordway. Caught him around the chest. They both tumbled down the stairs. Marco ran after them, barking. He leapt onto Ordway, knocking him off balance, so that he couldn't struggle to his feet.

Ordway's leg caught between two of the banister uprights. One splintered. He bellowed as his knee snapped. He slid to the bottom of the stairs and lay still.

Ordway clutched his knee, moaning.

Marco danced around Ordway's head. He barked and snarled.

Cole picked Marco up and held him to his chest.

"It's okay, Marco, we're safe now."

Marco Diary Entry 27

I'm wearing a black bandana around my neck. Elena wears a black dress and black high heel shoes. Her black veil does not quite hide the tears that stream down her face. I can't reach her right now or I would lick those tears away.

I stand next to Cole. Tony stands beside Elena. Shannon and Nicholas stand on the other side of the deep hole where men have lowered a big box. Javier's body is inside it. Everyone wears black. Everyone is silent.

After a while we all walk back to a big black car that takes us home to our compound. Cole and I go to our house, while Elena goes to hers, and Shannon and Nicholas go to theirs. Cole puts on tan shorts and a bright yellow shirt with big red flowers. He removes the black bandana and puts my red collar around my neck.

In the kitchen he gives me crunchies in a bowl next to my pillow and refills my water dish. He takes glasses from a cupboard, puts them on one end of the long table beside lots of bottles of liquid he calls booze. He never offers me any of that.

He pours himself a half glass of an amber liquid and sits beside me on the floor. He leans against a cupboard door, and I crawl into his lap. He takes a deep breath, puts the glass on the floor, and kisses me on the top of my head. He doesn't say a word. I lick his face.

Nicholas opens the door. He's wearing baggy shorts covered in pictures of bright yellow birds, a t-shirt, and a white apron with lots of pockets. He crosses the room, looking at me and Cole. He smiles but says nothing. I wag my tail but stay with Cole. Nicholas takes platters of food out of the refrigerator and puts them on the other end of the table. Tiny tomatoes, bowls of olives, chunks of cheese and meat. He slices bread and puts the pieces in a big basket. He puts out a big bowl of roasted vegetables.

Shannon comes in carrying a newspaper. She has on a long flowing dress that's bright green, the same color as her eyes. She sits at the computer desk reading then rolls the chair close to me and Cole. She leans over and pats my head. I lick her fingers. She smiles.

Elena arrives hauling a big bucket of strawberries. She's dressed in her jeans and white t-shirt. She's washed her face and I don't see any tears. She puts the bucket of fruit on the table, picks up a handful of berries, and sits next to Shannon. I wag my tail at her. She leans over and gives me a berry. Oh boy.

Nicholas finishes putting things on the table. He sits at the end of the bench near us. He takes Shannon's hand and raises it to his lips and kisses it.

Shannon turns the newspaper around, so Cole, Nicholas, and Elena can see the headline. Cole sighs. I sniff the paper. I don't know what it says. I can't read.

"So, Ordway confessed," Shannon says. "To everything."

"Even killing the reporter?" I feel the rumble of Cole's voice in his chest. "Why would he do that? The police never suspected murder."

"A guilty conscience?" Nicholas snorts.

"I don't see that." Shannon frowns.

"Protecting Krista, more likely." Elena pauses. "He seems like a fool."

"A fool for love. But cunning," Nicholas says.

"Does cunning require intelligence?" Cole asks.

"Sounds like the opening question of a Socratic dialogue." Shannon taps the table. "A trickster, anyway, but the jury's still out on the intelligence factor. He is certainly cunning, putting the castor beans into Donald's special blend, then hiding them in Javier's locker to throw suspicion on him, just in case. Finding Javier's phone in the locker and sticking it under the castor plant."

"All because Donald planned to force Krista to go with him," Cole interrupts. "But starting the fire. That was just stupid. Guaranteed to call attention to himself."

"Like I said." Elena's face crinkles. "Dumb or protecting Krista."

Shannon tilts her head to one side. "I don't think Krista has it in her. A victim of the kind of abuse she suffered rarely has the core strength to lash out. They're usually looking for a knight in shining armor."

"And Ordway donned the mantle." Nicholas sighs.

Everyone is quiet again. I like this better. But I feel Cole draw in a breath. "What a family. Do you think Portia killed her mother?"

"Or Donald killed her." Nicholas says softly.

"Maybe. But any evidence is long gone." Shannon pauses.

"How did Irene know how Javier died?" Nicholas's voice is barely audible. Everyone is silent again.

"Friends in high places. A pipeline to the coroner." Shannon stands, putting the newspaper into a drawer of the computer desk. "Enough. We're done." She turns to Elena. "What do we do with Javier's money?

There's a long silence.

Elena shakes her head. "I don't want it."

"Let's keep it under the potting bench until you decide." Cole smiles. "We'll think of something."

A silent calm fills the room.

Good. Now we can get back to normal. Run in the forest hunting squirrel and rabbit and deer. Eat lots of good food. Weed the garden. Smell flowers. Pick more great food. Everyone is quiet. It's peaceful. This feels like home now.

Cole raises his glass. "Here's to the families we choose."

Acknowledgements

I owe an enormous debt of gratitude to my sister, Sarah Wadsworth. She is the leader of our clan-of-the-dog-people and encouraged me to make one of the best decisions of my life – adopting a sweet little lost dog. My fabulous husband and best friend, David Deardorff, the best partner in crime I could ever ask for, is by my side every day and does more for me than I can ever enumerate. I am deeply in debt to members of my writer's group – Rebecca Cantrell, Ben Haggard, David Deardorff, and Judith Heath – their dedication to our shared craft lifts me up and pushes me to do better work. Thanks to friends and family who support me in so many ways: Danielle Marshall, Ruth Murphy, Carol Graves, Elinor Gollay, Deya Terrafranca, and Betsy O'Neil. And, as always, I owe much to my agent, Regina Ryan, fountain of knowledge and guiding light. She has taught me more than anyone about book publishing and how to navigate a career as an author.

About the Author (s)

January 25 – a dreary, rain-soaked day in the Pacific Northwest of the USA. I sit in bed, waiting for the sun to rise – late as always at this latitude. It's my birthday and I'm feeling sorry for myself despite the full-spectrum lights and extra doses of vitamin D. I send a text to my sister complaining about my winter blues.

"You need a dog," she texts back.

"Good idea. But my allergies." I have been allergic to all mammals (except humans) for many years.

"Get a hypoallergenic dog. Like a poodle."

"I don't want to buy a designer dog. I want a rescue. And I hate going to shelters only to say I can't have THAT one. I want to rescue ALL of them."

Fifteen seconds later a text arrives with a link to a dog on Pet-Finder.

"I found your dog," my sister says.

Uncertain, I show the picture to David. A little white Bichon Frise.

"Oh . . . that's my dog!" He's excited.

"What do you mean?" I wonder if he's had a stroke or is living in a parallel reality.

"For the past two weeks I've been dreaming about a little white dog. Out in the garden with me." He points to the picture. "That's the dog!"

We applied to the shelter, were approved, and a month later we met the ferry from Whidbey Island. That's when we met Frodo. He'd been picked up by the dog catcher in Los Angeles County and it had taken a while to clear the hurdles and transport him to the shelter that had listed him on the island.

Within a week he'd assigned himself to handle security. He noticed anything out of place. A different color car parked in the neighbor's driveway, a tall echinacea that had blown over on a windy day, robins and crows pecking in the grass. These events were highly suspicious. They worried him. He investigated.

"So, I have my own little detective," I said as we patrolled our large fenced garden. Apparently pleased by the title, he wagged his tail at me. Thus, the Marco Mysteries were born.

Other Books by the Author:

Fiction:

Murder on Maui. An Emma King Mystery, Mystery Bay Publishing. Kindle Edition.

Place of Refuge. An Emma King short story, Mystery Bay Publishing. Kindle Edition.

Non-fiction:

What's Wrong With My Plant? (And How Do I Fix It?) Timber Press, 2009

What's Wrong With My Vegetable Garden?: 100% Organic Solutions for All Your Vegetables, from Artichoke to Zucchini Timber Press, 2011

What's Wrong With My Fruit Garden?: 100% Organic Solutions for Berries, Trees, Nuts, Vines, and Tropicals Timber Press, 2013

What's Wrong With My Houseplant?: Save Your Indoor Plants with 100% Organic Solutions Timber Press, 2016

What's Wrong With My Marijuana Plant?: A Cannabis Grower's Visual Guide to Easy Diagnosis and Organic Remedies Ten Speed Press, 2017

Find us at:

Kathryn Wadsworth:

Website: https://www.kathrynanddavid.com

Facebook: https://www.facebook.com/profile.php?id=100008348293724

Instagram: https://www.instagram.com/kathryn.wadsworth/

Email: kathryn@kathrynanddavid.com

Amazon Author: https://www.amazon.com/Kathryn-Wadsworth/e/B002J3NQIY

Kathryn and David Facebook: https://www.facebook.com/david.deardorff.108/

Mystery Bay Publishing:

Facebook: https://www.facebook.com/mysterybaypublishing/

Sample: Marco Mystery 2

Blast from the Past

Prologue – Ten years ago

Cole squinted into the wind. He braced himself as the ship yawed in the white-capped waves. Rollers that had travelled across the Pacific Ocean lifted the stern, ran the length of the boat, and moved on toward the entry to the Strait of Juan de Fuca.

He lifted his camera and framed the shot of Cape Flatttery – the northwestern most bit of land on the U.S. Mainland. He'd come on deck for this image for his last article on daily life aboard a naval vessel. Today was his last as a naval communications officer. Tomorrow, when this ship arrived in Bremerton, he'd leave the navy. He'd served his four years and was ready to pursue other adventures.

He'd grown up on a boat – sailing with his itinerant musician parents and his older sister. He'd gone around the world. Several times, in fact. He'd discovered that growing up at sea, never living in the U.S., made him a real misfit in college. When he dropped out, he thought the navy would be a better choice. Not so much. Even more out of place than at college

Now he couldn't wait to develop his invention and wander in nature – seeking solitude, quiet, and connection with the wild.

"Steele!" The commander's voice bellowed over the PA system.

Cole looked up and scurried toward the pilot house, the pitch and roll testing his sea legs.

The commander turned toward him as he entered. "I know you haven't worked security in a while." The commander sounded hesitant. She drew in a breath. "But get out there. See to those sailors prepping the ordinance to offload."

"Yes, Ma'am." Cole saluted.

The wind had strengthened, and icy rain lashed his face. *Oh great. Just what I need. A detail I haven't done in two years.*

Grabbing the railings with hands and feet, he slid down the ladder to the forward deck. Four seamen gathered around the sling rigged to lift small munitions onto the gurneys. These would be swung over the side to the tender steaming out from Indian Island.

The men glanced at Cole as they wrestled with a heavy cylinder. The guys seemed to know their business. Cole kept quiet. No need to disrupt their concentration. He stood in the lee of the crane, keeping out of the lashing rain as much as possible.

A line swung loose. Cole grabbed it, got it back under control. Seaman Thompson, the youngest man on the team, lurched toward Cole, grabbed the line, and went back to the task. Cole helped him pull the line toward a winch by the gangway, which remained steady. It was still lashed to the railing. Cole secured the line to a cleat and crossed to the other men. They wrestled with a crate of side-arms that had come loose and skidded across the deck.

Thompson shouted. Cole turned. One end of the sling rose thirty feet, dropping the other end of the missile toward the deck. The ship rose atop a steep wave. The mortar hit the deck.

The blast slammed the men backwards.

Marco Diary Entry 1

We're in the rose garden. Not the big Portland Garden up the hill from where we live. Our own rose garden. The one Cole and Elena made to honor Christine. She's the alpha female who died last year. I never met her.

This city celebrates roses every year in June. The Rose Festival they call it. I guess that's why they call it the City of Roses, or Rose City. They use both names. The city where I was born – where I lived with my first family until they moved and lost me – is called the City of Angels. I don't know why. While I was searching for my family, the dog catcher picked me, but I got away and ended up here. That's another story I'll tell you sometime. I haven't been back there since I moved in with Cole. I was only trying to evade the dog catcher, but now he's my best friend.

This year Elena persuaded Cole to open our garden to visitors during the festival. He didn't ask me. And it's a real headache. I need to be extra vigilant, since, as you may already know, I am Chief of Security.

We have lots of gardens in our compound. A few houses too. Cole and I live in the one at the top of our sloping property. Our house is the one furthest from the street. Nicholas, Cole's chef, and his wife, Shannon, lives in another. She's a lawyer and works somewhere else, not in our compound. Their house is behind the communal kitchen where we all gather for the meals that Nicholas prepares. Elena, who takes care of the gardens, lives just past the vegetable beds. That's what they call them, even though nobody actually sleeps there. Hmm, maybe the vegetables do. I never thought of that. A tall fence with one gate in front by the street and another gate in back by the ally surrounds the whole compound.

Since I am in charge of security, I do frequent perimeter checks. No one comes in or out without me checking on them. Luckily the back gate is locked today. Even so I am very busy. I must check the front gate and keep my eyes on the people walking through the grounds. I sniff each visitor. If they speak to me, I wag my tail. But then I have to move on. I am starting to get tired, so I sit next to the entrance to the rose garden, watching the visitors who walk past me.

A tall, muscular woman, wearing a white uniform, strides through the entry and into the garden. She looks like she runs and works out at the gym the way Cole does. Now she turns and heads straight for Cole. I follow. As she gets closer, Cole turns his head. His eyebrows rise.

"Commander Franklin." Cole gives her a casual salute.

"Cole, please." The woman extends her hand. "Long time, no see."

Cole ignores her outstretched hand and holds the salute instead. "Oh, sorry. I see you've made Captain now." He doesn't smile.

I am wary. He is usually friendly. I sniff the woman's leg and poke her calf with my nose. She needs to know I am watching her.

She tips her head to one side. "I thought we were friends."

"You did?" Now Cole smiles. "I wonder why."

"Guess I was wrong." Captain Franklin looks at Cole with sad eyes. "Can we talk?"

"Isn't that what we're doing?" Cole sighs and, without waiting for her answer, leads the captain away from the rose garden, into the vegetable garden where there are no visitors. I follow.

Chapter One

Cole stopped abruptly. Captain Franklin, apparently with reflexes still quick, avoided colliding with him. Frowning he squared his shoulders and pivoted to face her. His hands rested at his hips, bracing himself to hear what she'd come to talk about.

"I see you've done pretty well for yourself, sailor." She'd dropped her friendly overtures.

Cole stared. Not interested in telling her the story of his good fortune, making a bundle from the sailor's gear he'd invented. He figured she knew all about it – a flotation device that was as thin as silk, warm enough to prevent hypothermia, and excellent body armor to boot. Now, many naval vessels carried it aboard. His experimentation with chemistry had succeeded. So had his business venture – a chain of outdoor outfitters and organized ecotours. A life he'd loved until his wife died on one of the trips. Had Franklin heard about that?

"My condolences sailor. I am sorry for your loss." She answered his unasked question.

Cole nodded. He was also unwilling to tell her the story of his misfortune. "What can I do for you Captain?"

The woman stepped back "I wondered if you'd contacted or been in contact with Seaman Thompson lately?"

Cole squinted his eyes. "Can't imagine why I would have." He shook his head.

"He lives nearby." Franklin tilted her head to one side. "Houseboat up on the Columbia River."

"Hmmm. Didn't know that." Cole was curious. "How's he doing? Must be difficult to maneuver life on the water from a wheelchair."

"Not sure," she drew in a deep breath. "I'd like your help finding out."

Cole didn't trust the Captain. Wondered why she'd come to him. There were others who'd served with them, even some sailors under her command who'd known him. Cole was quite certain that two of the sailors on deck the day Thompson lost his legs still served aboard her ship. Why ask Cole?

"I won't ask you if you remember the accident with the preparation to transfer munitions that day." Franklin paused. "Clearly you do."

Cole nodded. It was a memory he tried to forget. "A horrific accident." It had been a relief to leave the ship and walk away the following day. He had no interest in looking back.

Franklin shook her head. "It was no accident, Cole."

22877221R00149

Made in the USA
San Bernardino, CA
19 January 2019